MADELEINE

By Caroline St. Vincent

ISBN 13 978-1492725169

ISBN 10 1492725161

Also available in Kindle edition

Table of Contents:

Chapter One – Dunners at the Gate

A hush fell over deClare castle.

The sun poured down the sides of the bleached stone walls. Shadows cast from the turrets threw dark squares across the expanse of the bailey. It was not a time of day meant for hushing, but bustling and hustling. Yet, every member of the household stood silent, listening.

The booming voice came again.

"Open the gate, Baroness. You cannot dodge me forever. I came for my silver and I'll not be leavin' without it."

Inside the bower, the Baroness deClare twisted a handkerchief in her hands.

Her daughter, Madeleine, said, "What shall we do? Have you got any coins?"

"No, Madeleine, I do not. And that beast knows I have not."

Madeleine hated silver. It seemed to her it was necessary for everything and there was never enough of it.

The man at the gate yelled again. "Baroness. Be reasonable, now. You keep carryin' on like this and it'll be the debtor's prison for you and your daughters."

The Baroness sank onto the window bench.."

"Now Baroness," the voice yelled, "P'raps we can work something out. You know me to be a widow; the fever took my Mary a twelve month back."

"The impudence!" the Baroness cried. "As if I would marry that thieving scoundrel."

"It's only respectable I marry again," the man shouted on, unable to hear the Baroness' opinion on the matter. "P'raps I could take one of your daughters off of yer hands. One less mouth to feed and all that."

The Baroness looked startled. Then she eyed Madeleine.

"Absolutely not," Madeleine said.

Her mother shrugged and asked, "What are we to do then?"

"I shall rid the castle of that man this instant," Madeleine said. She bound her long red hair up with an old ribbon and strode from the room.

Madeleine ran down the curving stone stairs, nearly knocking over her sister. "Careful, Madeleine", Juliana said, rearranging the brass circlet that was nearly lost in her blond curls. "And do something about that odious man at the gate."

Madeleine called over her shoulder, "Perhaps you could do something on occasion, if you were not primping your curls all day."

Madeleine did not wait for Juliana's retort. She did not have time and Juliana's retorts were never very clever. Madeleine raced into the great hall and produced a small iron key from the purse tied around her waist.

It was the only key to a cupboard that nobody cared about. They did not care about it because they did not know anything of value was in it.

When Madeleine had first realized that her family faced financial difficulties, she had secreted anything of value she could into the cupboard. She did not think of it as stealing, exactly. She felt it was more saving her mother from herself. Madeleine knew that if she had not hidden these things they would be long sold, rather than waiting at the ready for truly dire circumstances.

Madeleine yanked open the cupboard. It was not nearly as full as it had been two years ago. There had been other days like today. Her mother and sister never inquired too closely about how Madeleine fended off the more insistent creditors. Her mother seemed satisfied to think it was Madeleine's sharp tongue that did the job. But Madeleine had discovered through experience that a combination of her sharp tongue, something of value and a dose of violence was what was needed.

Praise the saints, there were still a few good pieces left. She grabbed a heavy silver candlestick and ran out of the great hall.

Madeleine's second stop was the privy. She hated to go anywhere near it unless she was quite desperate, but today she needed the slop bucket.

She paused for a moment when she realized that with the candlestick in one hand and the slop bucket in the other, she would have no extra hand to hold her nose against the smell. Godfrey had told her that her father said the mark of courage was not what you did while the world watched, it was what you did when nobody was looking.

"Courage," she whispered.

She opened the rickety privy door and pulled the bucket out as fast as she could. Urine splashed over the rim and she felt bile rising in her throat.

"Now, Baroness," the voice boomed, "it would not be sellin' yer daughter for a debt, mind. I might not be a nobleman, but I'm respectable for all that."

Madeleine took a deep breath and charged up the stone stairs that led to the top of the keep's walls. She ran along the top of the castle walls until she came to the stone slab she was looking for.

The main entrance to the keep had an outer portcullis, open during the day, leading to a long rectangular room with a gate at the other end. Blessedly, the inner gate was locked. The roof of the rectangle, which Madeleine now stood on, was littered with murder holes. Should an enemy attack and breach the bailey walls, they could be picked off with arrows. Or, in this case, urine.

Madeleine crept to the hole directly over the inner gate and peered down. She saw a mass of sticky, dirty hair sprouting from a very round head that bobbed atop an even rounder body. "Disgusting," she whispered.

The head whipped around at the sound and she pulled back.

"Baroness, I'm just askin' for what be owed me. I know ye be in there."

Madeleine poured the bucket through the hole.

A yell, higher in pitch than Madeleine would have expected from a man, echoed off the stone walls.

"What the devil!"

Madeleine peeked down the murder hole. The big, round head with dirty hair was no longer there. She ran to the outer wall and looked down on the bailey.

The man shook himself and sputtered and wiped his eyes. His nag seemed equally offended and pawed at the ground.

Madeleine raised the candlestick and threw it as hard as she could.

It whirred through the blue sky and hit the man squarely on the shoulder. He cried out again and fell to the ground.

She called, "That, sir, is payment. Remove yourself immediately and never return."

The man staggered up and squinted against the sun to the top of the wall. "She-devil! I'll see you in prison yet."

"You shall do no such thing. You have been paid. If you wish to ask the constable whether he prefers the word of Lady Madeleine deClare or a scoundrel like yourself, that is your affair."

The man picked up the candlestick and scrutinized it. "Maybe I been fully paid, maybe I haven't. Maybe a high and mighty miss like yerself will come sorry someday for insultin' me."

Madeleine leaned over the keep wall. "Shall I fetch my bow and arrow?"

The man paused, as if to think through how likely it was that the Baroness' daughter would shoot him. Then he looked down at his urine-stained doublet. "Yer haven't seen the last of me, girl. No. Yer haven't."

Madeleine turned and stalked away. She did not know if she had seen the last of him or not. But she felt sure she had seen the last of him for that day at least.

She ran up the stairs to the bower to let her mother know that all was well.

The Baroness lounged on the heavily cushioned window bench. "Has he gone?"

"Yes, he has gone". Madeleine threw herself on her mother's bed. "But what are we to do? We cannot go on like this or we truly will end in debtor's prison."

The Baroness shuddered. "Do not speak of it."

Madeleine propped herself up on her elbows. The afternoon light streamed through the glazed window over her mother's head. Madeleine had to squint to see her. She said, "But we must speak of it. Our difficulties will not disappear by not speaking of them. We must at least try to do something or we shall be ruined."

The Baroness didn't respond. She generally did not respond when talk turned to money.

"Mother. We must devise a plan. Could we not come to an agreement with a responsible steward? A room and food until the estate is back in order, then silver to be paid?"

The Baroness turned her face and stared out the window as if she'd gone deaf. All Madeleine could see were her light curls rolling over her narrow shoulder.

Madeleine felt hot anger swirling in her belly. She said, "I have watched the tenants take their produce to market. They sell it, then they claim their crops failed and they cannot pay. Do not you see? They take advantage of us since father died. We are being driven to ruin and only a proper steward can put things to right."

In a quiet voice, the Baroness said, "And where would I find such a person?"

Madeleine was exasperated. "I do not know. Write to my Uncle. Perhaps he will know."

At the mention of her brother, the Baroness turned and sat up on the window bench. "You well know what my dear brother would advise. You could solve our problems quite easily if you wished."

"It would not be quite easy to marry Alfred," Madeleine said. "My cousin is a buffoon."

Madeleine knew her mother wished with all her heart that she would marry Alfred. The Baroness did not admire him, far from it. She did not believe Alfred would make her daughter a good husband. He certainly would not. The Baroness wished it because it was an easy solution. Upon the marriage, her brother would pay to fix the estate.

The Baroness was not accustomed to being troubled. She was the only daughter of a rich merchant and had been sheltered from every care. Madeleine's father had treated her as a delicate flower whose every perturbance was cause for alarm.

Now, a widow with two grown daughters and a failing estate, the Baroness did as she had always done. She waited for someone else to put things to right.

6

Madeleine stuck her chin out. "I would as soon go to debtor's prison. The company would be less repellant."

Before the Baroness could answer, another male voice shouted at the gate. "The Baroness deClare and the Lady Juliana deClare!"

The Baroness clutched at the folds of her faded silk gown. "Will they never leave us be?"

"Why does he call for you and Juliana?" Madeleine asked. "Usually they only ask for you." She narrowed her eyes. "The two of you didn't slip away and convince someone to give you credit for something frivolous, did you?"

"Do not presume to interrogate me, Madeleine. Just make him go away."

Madeleine sighed. She retraced her steps back down to the cupboard, grabbed a silver chalice, stopped at the privy and filled the slop bucket, trudged up the stone stairs and peered down the murder hole.

A man in blue and silver livery stood at the gate. He was far better dressed than most of their creditors. Madeleine wracked her mind to work out what debt he had come to collect. She gave up. Her mother bought things on credit whenever she wasn't being watched. Her mother's ideas of necessities were more expansive, and expensive, than most peoples.

Madeleine hauled up the slop bucket and poured it down the murder hole.

A deep voice cried out, "By the saints!"

Wearily, Madeleine went to the wall overlooking the bailey. The man was pulling off his urine-soaked doublet and cursing.

She heaved the silver chalice at him. It knocked him on the head and he fell to the ground.

The man staggered up and squinted at the top of the wall.

Madeleine called, "You have been paid, sir. Leave this instant and never return."

The man gave her a baleful look. To her surprise, he threw the chalice back up to her.

She snatched it from the air. What could he mean by it? Was he refusing the chalice as not valuable enough? That had never happened before. .

The man bowed and held forth a rolled parchment. "A communication for the Baroness deClare and Lady Juliana deClare from the honorable Earl of the house of Beaumont."

Madeleine gasped as she realized her mistake. He was not a creditor. He was the servant of an earl. A rather famous earl renowned for his skill in battle.

She took a deep breath. "Sir, I am afraid there has been a misunderstanding. I took you for...for...well, for someone else."

The man's face indicated that 'misunderstanding' was somewhat of an understatement.

Madeleine forced herself to smile. "Please wait a moment. I shall open the gate."

She scrambled down the stairs and unhinged the lock. It creaked open on rusty hinges.

The servant held the parchment out to her.

Madeleine's hands shook as she took the parchment. She said, "Do come in and refresh yourself. I shall have cook prepare you a meal. And you are welcome to stay until the morrow. And of course I shall do something about your doublet."

The servant curtly bowed. He said, "My visit to deClare castle has been delightful. I could not bear another moment of such happiness."

Madeleine felt herself bristle. Then she got a whiff of his doublet and thought perhaps he did have cause to be rude.

"Well," she said in a hopeful tone, "no need to trouble anyone else, such as the earl, about this silly misunderstanding."

The servant sniffed and turned on his heel. He called over his shoulder, "I keep nothing from the earl."

Madeleine's heart sank. She did not know why the mighty Earl of Beaumont would write to them, but she couldn't help thinking he would not wish urine thrown upon his servant.

Madeleine replaced the silver chalice in the cupboard and took the parchment up to the bower. She had decided it would be best not to mention that she had insulted the messenger.

She briefly considered whether or not this was lying. Madeleine didn't fool herself about it, she knew perfectly well that omission was just as bad as telling an untruth outright. So it was lying. On the other hand, her mother didn't hold up well under any sort of bad news. If her mother didn't need to know it, which she did not at the moment, it would be a kindness that she not be told.

The Bower was silent. Madeleine felt her voice sounded over-loud as she said, "Mother, it was not a creditor, praise God. It was a messenger from the Earl of Beaumont."

The Baroness had been lounging on the window bench with her usual dreamy look. She jumped up as if someone had taken a switch to her. "The Earl of Beaumont! Bring it here. Quickly."

Madeleine crossed the bower. The Baroness snatched the parchment from her hand and quickly unrolled it. As she read, color flamed into her cheeks.

The Baroness flung herself on the cushions of the bench with more energy than Madeleine had ever seen from her. Her eyes were sparkling and watery. "We are saved. I knew it. We are saved."

Madeleine could not imagine what could be in the parchment that would save them from financial ruin. Surely an earl they had never met had not written to say he was sending them silver. Madeleine said, "May I read it?"

Her mother handed her the parchment. The Baroness softly laughed and whispered, "I knew it, I knew we should be saved."

Madeleine read the message.

To the Baroness and Lady Juliana deClare,

Greetings from Henry Beaumont, Earl of the House of Beaumont. It has recently been communicated to me that we are distant relations. I beg forgiveness that I had been unaware of this until this late date. I have been remiss in recognizing my dear cousins and would consider it an honor to establish the connexion. I would propose a visit by myself and my respectable friend Sir Richard Langdon, should you forgive me my long inattention. I await your wish on this matter.

Respectfully,

Henry Beaumont

Madeleine read it again, searching for the part that saved her family. As far as she knew, creditors cared little about who you might be related to, distant or otherwise. She said, "What does this signify? He wants to recognize us as distant relations. How does this help us?"

A small smile was on the Baroness' lips. "That is not what it says at all, Madeleine. What it says is the earl has heard of Juliana's beauty and has come to seek a wife. With Beaumont's money, deClare castle will be glorious once more."

Had her mother gone mad? Did she so wish for their problems to go away that she read things that simply weren't there? Madeleine usually let her mother believe whatever small unreality she pleased, but this could not be allowed to go on. "Mother, the letter says no such thing. There is no mention of Juliana's beauty or wanting a wife."

The Baroness looked at Madeleine as if she were simple. "Of course, he does not directly say it. That would be ridiculous. However, his meaning is clear enough."

Madeleine was not convinced. She did not see how he at all implied he was coming to marry Juliana.

The Baroness cried, "My goodness! Here I am lying around as if I don't have a thousand things to do. Fetch me a parchment and ink. And call the seamstress, we shall need new gowns."

"I shall fetch you the parchment and ink. But you know we have not silver for a seamstress." Madeleine said.

"Do not be ridiculous, Madeleine. The price must be found. We cannot receive the earl in these old rags."

"The price cannot be found. We simply do not have it."

The Baroness stared hard at her. "You must think me a dolt, my dear. I do not claim to know where you have hidden valuables, though I have looked hard enough on occasion. But you cannot possibly think I believe you rid us of creditors simply by telling them to go away. I do not know what you have or where you have it, but something must be produced. We must have new gowns."

Chapter Two – Godfrey and the Goose

Madeleine felt her breath catch. She had never guessed her mother had known she had hidden anything. And the Baroness had looked for it! Thank the saints it had not been found. This would be a loss they could ill afford, but Madeleine could see her mother was resolute. There was nothing for it, she would have to give up one of their silver saviors for new gowns.

"As you wish," Madeleine said.

Madeleine gathered parchment and ink from the dusty steward's office that had not been used since her father died. She had sometimes come in to examine the accounts laid out on the table in the hope that she might be able to act as steward herself, but she could never make anything out of them. She did not doubt she could do it if it were taught her, but she did not seem to be able to teach herself. The last time she had sat at the old oak desk, the numbers had seemed to float around every which way and she had held her head in despair. She had never come back.

The door creaked as she closed it behind her. Madeleine paused in a passageway to be certain no one was about. She would have to be especially careful about the cupboard in the great hall from now on. Should her mother discover it and manage to break the lock, the deClare's ruin would come all the sooner.

The great hall was empty. Madeleine had dim memories of the hall in her father's time. Then, it seemed to her, it was never empty. In the evenings, a great fire roared in the grate and her father's friends sat at the top of the table. The lower half of the table was filled with pilgrims who told their tale for a night's food and lodging and entertainers of every sort. Even during the day, when many in the castle were out, there were stragglers in the hall and old hunting dogs slept near the fire or nosed through the rushes for what morsel might have been dropped the night before.

Those days had been over for many years. The hall now sat lonely and quiet, it's only company the dust motes that danced in front of the glazed windows. The family no longer spent their evenings there. It seemed too lonely with only three people and it was easier to heat the bower.

Madeleine listened carefully. Hearing nothing, she quietly opened the cupboard and pulled out the silver chalice that had been such an unfortunate weapon an hour before. "What a waste," she whispered. "A perfectly good chalice given up for silly gowns."

The chalice had been pawned, fabric bought and the seamstress called. Juliana and the Baroness had been in high spirits, their heads continually together debating colors and velvets and silks. Madeleine, in an effort to conserve some of the silver from the chalice, had argued that she did not need a new gown. The Baroness had declared she would not allow the Earl to see any daughter of hers walking around in rags.

The Baroness tugged at the hem of Madeleine's new gown, as if that might make it longer. Her mother sighed as she smoothed the creases from the velvet kirtle. "The seamstress was here a mere fortnight ago. How extraordinary you could have grown so much in that time. When will it end, I wonder?"

A small sigh escaped the Baroness, the sigh often associated with Madeleine. "Praise the Saints," she said, "your teeth are good and your mind sharp. That is something. It is only a pity you do not resemble your sister."

Madeleine gritted her teeth. "She has your looks mother, and that is well."

The Baroness gazed out the narrow leaded windows of the bower. "So she does. I wonder at my having married a red-haired man, God rest his soul. But then, he was rich and my father recommended him. I simply thought my daughters would favor me."

Madeleine looked up under the dark lashes framing her green eyes. "God presents mysterious challenges, does he not?"

Her mother's lips pressed together, in that peculiar way they did when she was cross. "Pray watch your tone, Maddy. It does not do you credit."

Madeleine thought there were entirely too many things that did not do her credit.

The Baroness turned from the window, her elegant figure silhouetted in the weak winter sun. She pointed a pale, slim finger at Madeleine. "I expect you to act the lady you are when Lord Beaumont arrives. Your sister's happiness depends on it."

Madeleine flopped down on the heavy cushions of the window bench, assuming she need not act the lady until the Lord had absolutely arrived. "Not that I will miss her, but why is Juliana so certain she will like this fellow? And so certain he will like her?"

"Juliana will like him because Earls are not falling from the trees in Petitshire."

Madeleine sank back into the brocade pillows and stared at the oak rafters of the bower. In a gay tone she said, "Does a day go by when we do not hear of her dew-kissed skin, her azure eyes, her golden hair, her untold grace? It can only be hoped her admirers never discover she uses the privy like other mortals. Though perhaps they would proclaim it reeks of roses."

A flush crept across the Baroness de Clare's perfect white cheeks. "That is quite enough. You need not degrade every conversation. Though I know you do it to vex me."

Madeleine jumped up from the window bench and hugged her mother's narrow shoulders. She whispered, "Truly, I do not."

Her mother's face relaxed.

Madeleine said, "Mother, I know this will vex you, but it must be said. I do not think you should pin so much hope on this Beaumont. He has promised nothing, and it may all come to nothing."

The Baroness' face darkened, as it had every time in the last fortnight that Madeleine had tried to make this particular point.

"Please mother, I only ask that we not assume our problems are solved. We do not know it yet."

The Baroness threw up her hands. "Why must you always endeavor to drag my spirits to the gutter? Why can you not be more like Juliana? She is not moping and predicting disaster at every turn. She is happy and carefree, just as a young lady should be."

Madeleine felt her face grow hot. Few things angered her more than being unfavorably compared to her silly sister. They were compared enough on their looks; Madeleine could not bear a comparison on their character. She said, "If I were more like Juliana, we would all be happy and carefree in debtor's prison."

The Baroness groaned. "Enough. Leave me. Lord Beaumont arrives this night and I have much to consider."

As Madeleine left the bower her mother called, "Pray, check the kitchens; all must be perfect."

Madeleine wove through the narrow stone passageways of the keep, not needing to hold up her kirtle as it was already too short.

She tripped into the yard. The cold winter light showed everything overly bright and there was a heightened sense of hurry in the air. The chambermaids were a whirlwind of giggles and whispers;

the laundress especially loud and red-faced. The stable boy strutted like a rooster, shouting orders in a voice that had grown deeper overnight. Even the chickens seemed convinced there was more cause for hysteria than usual and squawked as if they were headed directly to the dining table.

The only inhabitant who remained unchanged was Cuthbert, the old beggar. He crouched in a sunny corner of the yard, his back resting against the stone wall.

Madeleine made her way over to him, dodging chickens and horse dung. "Cuthy, how is it with you this day?"

Cuthbert peered up at Madeleine and smiled. It was a smile that held far fewer teeth than was generally expected. "A deal better now I sees your shinin' face. But as the facts stand, none too good. A steady sitchy-ation continues to elude. Leadin' me to the unfortunate lot of havin' to depend on the kindness of my fellow Adams and Eves."

Madeleine burst out laughing. "Do you imply you have looked for a steady situation?"

Cuthbert said, "I never did say 'look.' I said 'elude.' Entirely a different matter, Lady M."

Madeleine nodded. "So it is. Go see Godfrey later. I shall see you get some supper."

Cuthbert shook his head. "I won' wanna see him later." He lowered his voice. "On account a he be on the other side of a few drops of ale."

Madeleine started. "He is not…he did not…not today…"

"That he be, on this very day. Drunk as a Lord."

Her heart sank. She whispered, "Why today?"

Madeleine raced across the yard to the stone building that housed the kitchens. She poked her head in the doorway. Pots were meant to be boiling, meat roasting on spits, bread baking and servants running. But the kitchen was silent. Three of Godfrey's

17

scullions stood close together in a corner, looking uncertain. Then she heard Godfrey.

"I'll not do everything 'round here. I ain't a serf. Not nobody, not even a high and mighty Baroness, is gonna pile on the work and expect I say nothing of it." Godfrey leaned back in his chair and waved a long knife unsteadily around his head. "I'm the cook. Now I'm the steward, too? With no extra silver, thankee. What next? Wet nurse?" He snorted.

Madeleine cried, "Godfrey! What have you done?"

"I done nothin,' that be the whole truth of it." He laid the broadside of his knife along his nose. "I s'pose we be seein' what happens 'bout that."

"Oh, Godfrey. You know we cannot afford a steward as well as a cook just now."

"Can't ye now? I don' see the seamstress goin' without work. No, not her. You and your sister and the Baroness all struttin' round in new gowns." Godfrey paused and wiped the tiniest tear, if one had really been there at all, from a blood-shot eye. "Poor old me worked to death."

Madeleine knelt at Godfrey's knee. "I tried to prevent them from wasting money on new gowns, but I could not sway them. You know what is on their minds. Lord Beaumont comes today and they are convinced he will offer for Juliana's hand."

"He best be rich, then."

Madeleine stifled a giggle. "I am not as convinced as my mother that this Earl is intent on finding a wife. His letter did not indicate it."

"Another of the Baroness' crazy ideas, is it?," Godfrey slurred.

"I'm afraid it is." Madeleine glanced at the table piled with un-plucked fowl and unformed dough. "Nevertheless, an Earl is set to arrive at deClare castle and we have a duty to receive him properly."

Godfrey blinked. He reached over to the basin and threw cold water on his face. He dried himself with his dirty apron, leaving a trail of brown streaks on his cheeks. "I s'pose he be used to fine suppers."

"Very fine, I expect." She patted Godfrey's knee. "But come, do not be afraid of an earl."

Godfrey staggered out of his chair. "Earl or churl, I ain't afraid. There ain't a mortal man what spooks the likes of me. I reckon I be the best cook in all Danglen, thankee."

Madeleine thought that particular reckoning was a bit hopeful. Even sober, Godfrey was not a particularly good cook.

Godfrey grabbed a plucked goose from the table, held it by the beak and swung his knife at its neck.

Blood spattered in all directions. Madeleine jumped back, but she was too late. Droplets of blood dripped down the front of her gown.

She stared down at the scarlet rivulets seeping into the pale velvet. Godfrey whispered, "God's wounds."

Madeleine was momentarily speechless. Visions of her mother's face, twisted in horror, ran through her mind.

Godfrey said, "There be no gettin' out bloodstains. I reckon you dye the whole thing brown. 'It's my experience blood dries darker. Funny thing, that."

"Funny," Madeleine sputtered. "What have you done? I could strangle you!"

Godfrey backed away from her until he was as close to the fire as he could safely get. "Now that don't seem fair, talkin' of murder when it be an accident."

Madeleine took a deep breath. "I must run and change to my old kirtle. I shall think of something to tell my mother. But you, Godfrey, must take care of this supper!"

Godfrey glanced at Madeleine's ruined gown and shuddered. "Least I can do." He turned to his scullions. "What you be doin' standin' there like addlepated ninnys? Fires up, meat roastin,' bread in the ovens!"

Madeleine tore out of the kitchens and raced across the yard. She flew past Cuthbert, her long auburn hair flying behind her. He called out, "Has that no account drunkard accosted you, M'lady?"

Madeleine didn't answer Cuthbert. She jumped through the doorway into the keep. As she ran across the great hall, her mother's voice stopped her in her tracks.

"Madeleine, may I present Lord Beaumont."

Chapter Three - Lord Beaumont and Sir Richard

Madeleine slowly turned around. Her mother and sister stared at her. Her mother's face was tight with anger and her sister's cheeks scarlet. Next to them stood a man of twenty or so, tall and broad-shouldered, with golden hair cropped close. His face was brown, as if he spent much of the time outdoors, and his dark blue eyes sparkled. She smiled at him, until she noticed his smile had something of a sneer in it. She glanced over at his companion. He was shorter and darker, with a stocky build. He stared into space over Madeleine's head.

Madeleine gathered her wits and curtsied.

Lord Beaumont bowed. He said, "Have you by chance murdered someone?"

"I attempted it, but the blackguard escaped," Madeleine said.

"Madeleine!" the Baroness cried.

A scullion, who had been pressed into service as a page, snickered in a corner of the hall.

Lord Beaumont raised a brow. "May I present my companion, Sir Richard Langdon."

Sir Richard bowed low, his shoulders shaking in silent laughter.

Madeleine curtsied, though she felt she would rather knock the smirks off both of their faces.

Juliana patted her blond curls. "I am sure my sister has a perfectly respectable reason to have blood on her gown. Pray tell us, Madeleine, what misfortune has befallen you?"

Madeleine said, "It was not as serious as it looks. It was merely the untimely meeting of a goose and a knife. Entirely survivable, I believe."

Juliana looked as if she'd like to say something sharp, but did not dare in front of the earl.

The Baroness stepped forward. In a cool tone, she said, "Madeleine, dear, let us retire to the bower." She gripped Madeleine's arm and marched her from the hall.

In the bower, the Baroness was silent for a moment. She clenched and unclenched her small white hands. In a low voice she said, "What in the saints' names has happened in the kitchens?"

Madeleine attempted a breezy tone. "All is well. It was merely a silly accident."

The Baroness looked into Madeleine's eyes. "Is he drunk?"

Madeleine looked up at the rafters, as if there were something interesting up there. She said, "Is who drunk?"

"Godfrey," the Baroness said. "Is he drunk?"

"No," Madeleine said. "Godfrey is perfectly fine, he--"

"If he ruins this supper," the Baroness said, interrupting Madeleine, "I shall see him out the bailey gate by dawn."

Madeleine cupped her mother's tiny, heart-shaped face in her hands. "Supper shall be lovely – roasted goose, lamprey tureen, baked apples, fresh bread. It smells delicious."

The Baroness sighed. "It had better." She pulled herself away and examined Madeleine's kirtle. "That is quite ruined. Change to your old one, tattered as it is." She glanced around the bower with a look of exasperation. "Pray, where is Agnes? How is it her only talent is being elsewhere when she's looked for?"

"Never mind, I can dress myself. Return to our guests. Poor Juliana must be in a state having to entertain an earl on her own."

"Juliana does not have 'states.' Still, it is unseemly she be without a chaperone. Be not long and, for heaven's sake, Madeleine, let this be the last embarrassment."

Her mother gathered the train of her gown and glided from the room. Madeleine turned and caught her own reflection in the looking glass. Her heart sank. A too tall girl in a too short, blood-spattered gown.

How ridiculous she must have appeared to Lord Beaumont. The idea made her cheeks burn, which made her angry. Why should she care? She wasn't to be foisted upon him. The earl could not possibly concern himself with an awkward sister-in-law. Then Madeleine thought about the supper and prayed Godfrey would somehow manage it to their credit.

Madeleine scrambled out of her gown and slipped into her old one. It was, of course, too short. The front skimmed her ankles shamefully and the train barely rested on the floor. The velvet was worn at the elbows, and worse, where she sat on it. Madeleine straightened the brass circlet atop her head and glanced into the looking glass. Her red hair gleamed against the faded blue velvet and her green eyes seemed unnaturally bright.

She felt she couldn't look worse. Fifteen and still growing. Madeleine thought it would be a wonder if someday her head did not pop right through the rafters.

Madeleine somehow managed to enter the great hall with some dignity and converse with Lord Beaumont and Sir Richard without further embarrassment. She found it difficult not to stare at the earl. He was by far the tallest man she had ever seen. Madeleine's head reached just to his shoulders. She thought Juliana, as petite as she was, looked like a tiny faerie standing next to him.

The Earl spoke easily on a variety of subjects. Madeleine would be almost jealous of Juliana's good fortune, except, she could not quite like the man. His words were formal and polite, and yet there was a tone to them that made her feel laughed at.

Madeleine glanced uneasily at the far side of the hall. Godfrey's scullions were running to and fro, laying down the delicately carved nef boxes that held their napkins, knives and spoons.

Lord Beaumont watched as well, with an amused smile. She wondered if he noted they did not employ a bevy of pages to lay the table.

Godfrey appeared, framed in the servant's archway that led out to the kitchens. He swayed and caught himself on the doorframe. Madeleine felt her stomach flip. By the saints! How much had he drunk after she left him? He could not mean to act as steward in his state.

But Madeleine saw that was exactly what Godfrey was bent on doing. He tugged at his stained surcoat and put a foot unsteadily forward. He cleared his throat. "Supper…is served." Madeleine heard him mutter, "Such as it is."

Lord Beaumont gave his arm to Juliana, while Sir Richard escorted the Baroness. Madeleine was left to follow behind.

The Baroness glared at Godfrey as she was handed to her chair at the center of the trestle table. Lord Beaumont sat to the Baroness' left with Juliana at his other side. Sir Richard sat on the Baroness' right. Madeleine assumed she was meant to sit next to Sir Richard.

Madeleine peeked at Godfrey. He seemed pale and unsteady as he turned away to a side table to carve the meat.

The Baroness said, "Lord Beaumont, I understand you have just returned from the frontier. We have had vague reports of a victory at Fleur, but we receive sporadic news here. Can you tell us of it?"

Lord Beaumont set down his wine goblet. Before he could answer, Juliana said, "Pray do. We are most anxious to know what the Riadon women are wearing. We despise them, of course, but they do have a certain style."

A flicker of irritation crossed the earl's face.

Madeleine laughed. "In truth, if one must have enemies, it is well they are stylish. But perhaps we could hear of the actual siege of the city."

Beaumont turned to Madeleine. "King Conrad managed it brilliantly. Fleur was adequately defended, but their lead knight saw the hopelessness of holding out against us."

Sir Richard interrupted. "Do not be modest, Beaumont. It was you who managed it brilliantly. DeRichy saw the hopelessness of holding out after you explained it to him for two entire days."

Beaumont said, "DeRichy is an honorable man, despite being on the wrong side. He would not put the people who depend on him through unnecessary suffering." Beaumont paused and stared at his silver goblet. "DeRichy and I agreed that the sacrifice of innocent people had already been too much."

Godfrey leaned over Lord Beaumont's shoulder, swaying as he balanced a heavy silver platter.

Lord Beaumont leaned back to afford Godfrey room. Godfrey skewered a hunk of meat and plopped it on the plate meant to serve Beaumont and the Baroness.

Madeleine stared at the meat. The skin was roasted black and blistered, yet the meat appeared no more cooked than when the goose still lived.

A small smile crossed Lord Beaumont's face. "Charming."

The Baroness, her face descending into a dangerous shade of purple, said, "Godfrey, perhaps you will serve the bread. I trust it has been actually baked?"

Godfrey dropped the platter of goose onto the trestle table. He bowed unsteadily to the Baroness. "My worthy assistants will be servin' your most graciousness. I, meself, shall retire." He turned on his heel and wove from the hall. He bumped into the doorframe, said, "s'cuse me," and was gone.

Beaumont stared hard at the Baroness. "M'lady, do you allow your servants to disrespect you so?"

The Baroness dabbed at her eyes. "It is hard on a widow, M'lord. You haven't the first idea of what a woman must go through."

Lord Beaumont flushed and looked down at his plate. In a low voice he said, "I am certain it is difficult. Forgive me. Rudeness is inexcusable. Allow me to run that blackguard from the castle at first light."

"Run Godfrey out!" Madeleine cried. "He has been with us for more than twenty years. He is just, at this moment, indisposed."

Sir Richard laughed. "You mean disposed to the ale cask?"

"Oh, so what if he is?" Madeleine said. "He is a part of our household. You would propose we put him on the road to starve simply because he may be having…he is experiencing…a slight difficulty?"

Lord Beaumont said, "Describing this supper as a 'slight difficulty' is kind indeed. But loyalty should be respected and is in short supply in these times."

The rest of the supper, consisting only of bread and some cold meat one of the scullions brought in, passed quietly.

The ladies retired to the bower and left Lord Beaumont and Sir Richard over a chess board. As soon as they were out of earshot the Baroness stamped her foot. "That scoundrel! I shall murder Godfrey with my own two hands." She paced back and forth across the bedchamber. "Would that I convinced your father to get rid of that man twenty years ago. I knew from the first day he could not cook. Now he is a drunkard, too."

Madeleine sat on the window bench. "Do not be unreasonable, mother. He has been with us for those twenty years. And we have not paid him in months. Does he ever complain of it?" She had to suppress a smile. Godfrey complained bitterly to Madeleine on a daily schedule.

"I do not care, he has humiliated us for the last time," the Baroness said.

Juliana squeezed Madeleine out of the window seat. "This is a tiresome conversation. Did not you note that Lord Beaumont was interested in the company, not the repast? Did not you see him staring at me?"

The Baroness seemed to relax. She stroked Juliana's curls. "Indeed, it would have been hard not to note it. He seemed quite struck."

Madeleine thought they might be mistaken about the Lord's staring. He had looked at Juliana as if she were a dolt when she asked what the Riadon women were wearing. But then Madeleine remembered that her mother and Juliana were generally right about such things, and she was generally wrong. Before she could muse over Beaumont's inscrutable expressions any further, the Baroness' chambermaid burst in.

She sank into the awkward curtsy that always irritated the Baroness. "A messenger has come!"

The Baroness said, "Calm yourself, Agnes. It is not an extraordinary event." She stared at the maid, then sighed. "Seeing as a messenger has come, would there perhaps be a message?"

Agnes smirked and glanced at the parchment in her hand. In a saucy tone, she said, "Yes, M'lady, there be a message. I wonder at you not knowing it."

The Baroness held out her slim, white hand. "Give it to me and cease torturing me with your wonderings."

Agnes handed over the parchment with a careless curtsy. She left the bower mumbling, "Torture be a strong word, 'specially as I ain't been paid in my near recollection."

The Baroness unrolled the parchment and read its contents. She pressed her lips together and laid it on her lap.

Juliana said, "Well?"

"It seems your uncle cannot come to us. He has pressing business in Bellham."

Chapter Four – The Lord's Opinion

Juliana jumped up from the window bench. "Pressing business? What can be more pressing than negotiating with Beaumont for my hand? Has he lost his wits? What shall we do? Who shall speak for us?"

"Do not disturb yourself, my darling, lest you look a fright on the morrow. Your good uncle has not left us stranded. He sends Alfred."

Juliana gasped and sank down back down.

Madeleine almost felt a pang of pity for Juliana. Her cousin Alfred was empty-headed, yet thought he was a wit. He was proud without the slightest reason; he was everything disagreeable. The last time he had visited had been two blessed years ago. On that occasion, he had informed Madeleine he might condescend to marry her, depending on how she filled out as a woman.

Juliana's face was as red as a fall apple. "Mother. Uncle cannot be in earnest. He would hardly expect us to put ourselves in the hands of that nonsensical boy."

"Come, Juliana," the Baroness said, "Alfred was but sixteen when he visited last. A great deal may be accomplished, a great deal may change, between sixteen and eighteen. Especially for a man. I am certain my brother would not send him were it not so."

Juliana threw her blond curls over her shoulder with a petulant look. "It had better be so."

"And consider, my dear, through subtlety I can negotiate much myself. Alfred shall attend for the sake of appearance. He can escort Beaumont hunting and otherwise occupy the gentlemen during the day."

Madeleine giggled.

The Baroness looked at her sharply. "What amuses you, miss?"

"Pity poor Beaumont," Madeleine said, "doomed to spend whole days with Alfred. Even an earl cannot withstand such an assault."

Her mother narrowed her eyes. "You shall be cordial to Alfred. You may find he has something to offer you."

Madeleine did not answer. She knew her mother alluded to marriage. Madeleine suspected her mother and uncle had discussed it in detail. But Madeleine had said she would never marry him. She had even said she would rather enter a convent. Her mother had seemed to consider that the empty threat it was. Still, she would not do it. She simply would not.

The Baroness said, "Madeleine, before you retire it would please me if you spoke with Godfrey. I am not up to the task and Juliana needs her rest. Make it clear that if he has a drop of ale on the morrow, it shall be his last inside the confines of de Clare castle."

Madeleine wandered out of the bower and down the staircase toward the great hall. She took her time so she could think what to do with Godfrey. How could she separate Godfrey and ale? It had never been a matter of him not drinking, rather a matter of how much. It had always been so; she had heard tell of Godfrey being her own father's particular drinking crony.

Madeleine's father would escape being surrounded by females and creep out to the kitchens. He and Godfrey would sit in front of the hearth, drinking ale and solving the world's problems. Godfrey's wife Bertha used to say that after Madeleine's father died, Godfrey drank for two. But Bertha had herself died a year ago. Now it seemed Godfrey drank for three. How could Madeleine slow him down?

As she approached the great hall she heard Beaumont's voice. Madeleine paused before she reached the archway.

"I tell you, Langdon, this idea of my father's that I must marry before year's end is unaccountable."

Sir Richard laughed. "There is naught unaccountable there. His gout grows worse by the day. He wants the Beaumont succession secured before he departs the world."

"Nonsense," Beaumont said. "His body is as strong as an ox; it is his mind that's going. To insist I choose between the de Quincy girl and this de Clare girl? It is absurd; one is sillier than the other."

"But you are a distant cousin to both. A prudent choice; their backgrounds are known. And as far as silly? What matter?"

"What can you mean 'what matter'?" Beaumont asked.

"What I mean, friend, is it is wise to find mirth at your hearth and save your serious thoughts for your friends. Would you really have a wife as clever as yourself? For me, I would not prefer it."

"I do not understand you, Richard. How am I to countenance a dimwit like Juliana? What on earth would we speak of? And would I be plagued by long visits with her ridiculous family? Perhaps they would be kind enough to bring their talented cook along."

"Drink your wine, Beaumont, and forgo taking yourself so seriously. You really must, you know. Things are likely to worsen."

"How so?"

"I have had it from a servant that their cousin Alfred is due on the morrow. Apparently, he is the sparkling diamond on the de Clare's crown of silliness."

31

Madeleine heard Beaumont groan. Her cheeks burned. They were not as silly as that! Ridiculous family! Juliana a dimwit! And Madeleine not mentioned at all, not even noticeable enough to gather an insult.

She thought to charge into the great hall and confront the high and mighty Lord Beaumont. To shame him into taking back his words. Until she realized it would seem…ridiculous.

No. Madeleine could not have her revenge as she liked, but she would have it. She would tell Juliana and her mother. Madeleine supposed she would have to tell Alfred too. Then they would run that man out of the county.

Madeleine crept back down the passageway and slipped out the servant's door to the yard. The keep was quiet and glowed cold under a heavy moon. No soul stirred, not even Cuthbert. Madeleine guessed he had found a soft straw bed in the stables.

She peeked into the kitchens. Godfrey sat alone, staring into the hearth fire. She said, "Godfrey, are you all right?"

Godfrey looked up, his face puffy and eyes rimmed red. "A poor, forsaken soul like myself? Driven to drink through overwork, then my poor weakened body succumin' to the drink I been driven to? I'll be tossed into the cold world through no fault of my own. And my head hurts."

Madeleine suppressed a laugh. It had been her experience that the guiltier Godfrey felt, the sorrier for himself he felt. She sat down in front of the fire and patted his arm. "You'll not be tossed into the cold world, not this time anyway. And my head hurts as well. I have heard my family spoken of, and it was not flattering."

Godfrey sat up straight. "What man dares insult the great house of de Clare? I be rippin' 'em in two. I be roasting 'em on the fire. And then I be…demanding an apology."

Madeleine said, "As charming as the idea is of receiving an apology from a roasted, ripped in two man, I think it not practical. As it was the earl who spoke, the sheriff would be hard upon you."

Godfrey's shoulders slumped. "It be my fault, I reckon."

"Not entirely. Though a drunken cook could only add to our air of ridiculousness."

"Is that what he said? That you be ridiculous?"

"Oh, not me. I did not merit a mention. He spoke of my mother and Juliana. And you, of course."

"Don't worry 'bout me none. He just observed the unfortunate result of a pressured soul seekin' solace where he might find it. But miss, your mum and sister are a bit silly. Though I not be sayin' it outside the family and would gut the man wot notes it."

"I know, dear. My mother shall be terribly hurt when I tell her what Beaumont has said."

"Why you be doin' a thing like that?" Godfrey asked.

"Because Juliana cannot marry him!" Madeleine said. "The earl disdains her, Godfrey. His father pressures him to marry. If the earl succumbs to his father's pressure, poor Juliana! She does not see it now. But when it would be too late, she would feel his sting. And she would be miserable for it."

"But if she don't see it now, why should she ever? She ain't exactly the brightest star in the sky."

"She would see it. Juliana's nerves are stretched taut at the moment; she hardly hears what is said. But later, yes, she would. Despite his fair appearance, he is a cold, hard man. I must make my mother see that."

"I don' think telling the Baroness will solve the matter.

"Of course it shall. She will be furious."

"She would if she believed you. But it be my particular experience that a thing ain't believed when it don't wanna be believed. I reckon the Baroness would say you be dreamin' or imaginin'. Or jealous even."

"Jealous? Of that rude man?"

"I just say she might think that."

"Well that is just...he is the most...that is the stupidest thing you have ever said."

"Don't go gettin' your dander up at me. I reckon I done said a thousand things stupider than that. Bertha used to keep lists of 'em in her head and whip 'em out whenever she liked."

Madeleine sat staring straight ahead. In truth, she could not have explained why she was so angry.

Godfrey gave her a thoughtful look. He said, "You be sure this earl is a blackguard through and through? Ain't there nothing good about him?"

"Good? No. Nothing at all. He is horrible."

"Strange," Godfrey said. "The usual measure of a man is he be mostly good or mostly bad. Figurin' no one man is a saint or the devil his self."

"Oh Godfrey," Madeleine said. "you split hairs. That he may not be the actual devil, I will concede. His appearance is pleasing and he is intelligent and well-spoken. But those things cannot hide a black heart."

"And that be what you think? The earl has got a black heart?"

"The blackest." Madeleine said.

Godfrey considered this, then said, "I don' claim to have warm feelings for your sister. She's slung a few too many arrows in my direction. Still, she be harmless enough. I would not wish her a bad end. The earl will have to be gotten rid of."

Madeleine sat up, startled. "Godfrey! Do not even think of murder."

"Murder?" Godfrey cried. "You barmy lass. I ain't swingin' from the hangman's noose for nobody. No, what we got to do is help the man show his self for what he is."

"But how?" Madeleine asked.

"If he be as bad as you say, I got a mind opportunities will present themselves." Godfrey laughed. "I be guessin' if he thinks Juliana's silly, he'll make short work of your cousin Alfred."

Madeleine groaned. She had somehow managed to forget that Alfred arrived on the morrow.

Madeleine left Godfrey after wrenching a promise from him that he would not touch ale until the earl had left the castle. She did not think he would stick to it, but perhaps he would curb himself.

She crept past the great hall and up the stone stairs. Lord Beaumont and Sir Richard still sat before the massive stone fireplace. Much to Madeleine's relief, they were silent.

The bower was quiet. Her mother softly snored from the depths of her bedstead, while Agnes muttered in her dreams at the Baroness' feet. Madeleine crept into bed with Juliana and tried to sleep. Juliana kicked and turned and pulled the coverlet as if she resented sharing a bed.

Madeleine thought about what Godfrey had said. He was right, she was certain. The earl could not hide who he was for long. Madeleine had simply to help him show himself, to leave the crumbs for him to follow.

As she thought of this, she felt a pang of regret for what might have been, for the happiness Juliana might have found. Would that the earl's heart were as bright as his countenance. How was it that such darkness was hidden in such a breast? She thought he was like a brightly wrapped package full of happy promise. Until it was opened.

Chapter Five – A Courtship Falters

The following morning, Madeleine looked down on the garden from the bower casement. It was a tangle of weeds, broken branches and rotting apples; the gardener had been let go at the end of summer.

Juliana walked the path with Sir Richard. Her high laughter rang up to the window like a peal of church bells. Sir Richard leaned over and whispered in Juliana's ear. She shrieked and wagged her finger at his nose.

Madeleine leaned further out the window, breathing in the crisp morning air. She took in the rest of the garden. Ah, there he was. Monsieur Taciturn.

Beaumont stood, arms crossed, under the bare branches of the apple tree. Madeleine wondered that even this bright morning could not lift his spirits above a scowl.

"Madeleine. Close the shutters, it is cold enough in here."

Madeleine started. She had not heard her mother enter the bower. "Forgive me, I just observed our honored guests taking a stroll in the garden."

"The garden? How did we allow them into the garden? It is a disgrace."

Madeleine glanced out the window. "I imagine Lord Beaumont agrees with you."

The Baroness pushed Madeleine out of the way and peered out. "By the saints, this will not do. What does Juliana think of?"

"Very little in the gardening way, I presume."

"That is not my meaning. How is Beaumont left alone?" the Baroness asked.

"Perhaps the earl's countenance does not suit the light of morning. He is better matched to midnight." Madeleine said.

"Cease your idle ramblings, I've a headache already. Go to the garden this instant and rid it of Sir Richard."

"Rid the garden of a knight?" Madeleine asked, laughing. "How shall I do it? I have no lance."

The Baroness' face tightened. "Madeleine. Press me no more this day. Take Sir Richard to the stables. Or anywhere you like. Just get him out! Lord Beaumont and Juliana must have time to warm to each other."

Madeleine thought she might comment on the absurdity of Beaumont warming to anything, but decided she had said enough for one morning.

Madeleine wandered across the keep, not eager to reach the garden quickly. To the stables, indeed. On what pretence? To show Sir Richard their decrepit nag?

Madeleine reached the garden gate and peeked in, wondering how she might slip past Beaumont unnoticed. She was relieved to find he no longer stood under the apple tree.

She swung the gate open, its rusty hinges shrieking, and followed the gravel path. The box hedges had not been trimmed and leaned in, leaving just a narrow lane to travel through. Madeleine rounded a bend. Beaumont stood in front of her.

She felt herself flush and dropped down into a curtsy.

Beaumont bowed stiffly. "Lady Madeleine, do you take a turn in the garden?"

"Only to turn around and go out again, M'lord," Madeleine said in a light tone. "I have a mind to show Sir Richard our horse."

Beaumont wrinkled his brow. "I was not aware you kept a quality horse. I presume he was in use when we arrived."

Madeleine felt the sting of the barb, but merely said, "Presume as you wish."

Beaumont said, "I would be glad to accompany you."

"What?"

Juliana's voice sang out from around the bend. "Sir, I insist you never again compare my eyes to twilight. It is too impertinent!"

"Perhaps he referred to her mind," Beaumont muttered.

Sir Richard and Juliana rounded the bend. Sir Richard bowed to Madeleine. He turned to the earl. "Beaumont, where have you been hiding yourself?"

"I've not been hiding, Langdon. Simply enjoying the merits of a quiet garden."

Madeleine said, "The earl has not had a proper tour, I am woefully inadequate. Sir Richard, would you accompany me to the stables while Juliana shows Lord Beaumont the glories of the morning?"

Sir Richard bowed. Lord Beaumont looked startled, and then his face settled into a frown.

Juliana said, "I must warn you, Lord Beaumont, if you are as bold as Sir Richard I shall scold you without mercy."

Beaumont bowed. "I am warned."

Madeleine and Sir Richard walked across the keep to the stables.

"M'lady Madeleine," Sir Richard said. "I did not know you had a keen interest in horseflesh."

Madeleine smiled. "It would be hard, indeed, to have an interest in ours. But what of yours? Did you bring your war horse?"

Yes, always. Beaumont offered to stable him and lend me a destrier, but I never leave Glory behind.

Madeleine and Sir Richard entered the stables. The gloomy structure was only lighted here and there by shafts of sunshine sneaking through the slats of the pine board walls.

Sir Richard pointed proudly to a chestnut colored warhorse. The animal was broad in the chest and pawed at the fresh hay under its hooves.

Sir Richard rubbed the horse's nose. "Some would argue it, but I believe Glory is the best horse that ever lived."

"I would not argue it. And Glory must have the sunniest of tempers, to have the sunniest of owners."

Sir Richard looked away. "Ah, but the sun pales to some, does it not? Beaumont is a lucky man, to marry the sun living and breathing."

Had Sir Richard just said what Madeleine thought he had? That Juliana resembled the sun? No, that was too ridiculous. She said, "I believe your friend the Earl could benefit from sunshine."

"Ah," Sir Richard said. "You think him humorless. You are right to some degree. The earl does not laugh as easily as I do."

Madeleine was silent for a moment. Then she said, "I know it is rude to enquire, but how is it that you are friends with such a man? Beaumont is, well, he is so…disagreeable."

"He can be that, I know. But Beaumont is the best of men, once one has been through the painful process of getting to know him."

Sir Richard laughed. "When I was introduced to him, the first thing he said to me was 'may I ask where you acquired that accent.'"

"What did you say?" Madeleine asked.

"I said I'd paid twelve pence for it at market. A steep price, but the peddler had sworn it would annoy the house of Beaumont."

Madeleine burst out laughing. "And what did he say to that?"

"He excused himself and we have been friends ever since."

"It seems such an unlikely friendship." Madeleine said.

"Perhaps so. But Beaumont and I complement each other well," Sir Richard said. "He gives my thoughts weight when I would, in uncontrollable merriment, let them float to the sky. For myself, I give his thoughts lightness when he would, in uncontrollable seriousness, let them sink to the ground."

Madeleine did not know what to think. Sir Richard was a gentleman in every respect. But even with this reasoning, how could Sir Richard hold such a proud, disdainful man as the earl in high esteem? She said, "No matter, Sir Richard. I often enquire into things that cannot concern me. Perhaps Juliana shall see what I do not."

Sir Richard flinched. Then he forced a smile. "Beaumont is the only man I would admit to be deserving of your sister."

That afternoon Madeleine was forced to remain in the bower and attend to her sewing. Her mother had explained she would 'contrive' to leave Juliana and Beaumont alone. As the Baroness said, 'no man woos in front of an audience.'

Madeleine stabbed at her embroidery in frustration. If Beaumont were to move too quickly to secure Juliana's hand, she would have no chance to expose him until it was too late for her sister.

The Baroness breezed into the room. "It is done. Sir Richard is off on an errand and I have excused myself to deal with a pressing matter. The earl and Juliana are alone in the great hall."

Madeleine thought how she might get herself out of the bower. "Mother, it is not seemly Juliana be unattended. Surely, I should go down."

Her mother frowned.

"I should not be in the way," Madeleine said. "I should just be in the hall for propriety's sake."

"Madeleine," the Baroness said, "you hardly need instruct me on matters of propriety. I shall give Beaumont a quarter of an hour and then return myself."

They dropped into silence. Madeleine picked at a misplaced stitch under her mother's watchful eye. The Baroness had once pointed out that, as impossible as it was, Madeleine picked out more stitches than she put in.

After what seemed like an eternity, Madeleine said, "It seems we've been here half the day."

Before her mother could answer, Juliana burst into the bower. She stopped, stared at her mother for a moment, then heaved a sob and threw herself onto the bed. She mumbled something into the fur counterpane as her mother rushed to her side.

The Baroness stroked her hair and murmured, "There now, he has done it? Calm yourself and tell me all."

Juliana shuddered.

Madeleine's heart sank. That Beaumont would ask so soon! Here but a day and not even liking Juliana.

The Baroness said, "You are overcome with emotion, my love. It is only natural. Gather yourself and speak to me."

Juliana rolled over and hiccupped. "He did not ask me! He, I think he insulted me."

The Baroness raised her brows. "You are mistaken. Tell me what was said."

42

Juliana sat up. In a snuffling voice she said, "Well, we were standing at the window and I admired the view and he said nothing. So I could not think what to speak of next. Just then we saw Ralf, the cowherd's boy. So I said, 'that foolish boy once compared my hair to harvest wheat.'"

The Baroness leaned forward, listening intently.

"Then the earl said, 'foolish indeed.'" Juliana swiped at her eyes. "I did not know what to make of it. I laughed and said it was just a cowherd who would not know how to turn a pretty complement. And still the Earl said nothing. So I said, M'lord, what would you compare my hair to?"

Juliana burst into tears all over again.

The Baroness put an arm around her shoulders. "There now, out with it. What did he say?"

Juliana's shoulders shook and she took a deep breath. "He bowed and said, M'lady I am not gifted at inventing aimless compliments."

Madeleine bit her lip. Not only had he not wooed Juliana, he seemed to require no assistance in getting rid of himself.

Juliana threw her handkerchief on her lap. "Why can he not be like Sir Richard? Gay and chivalrous and everything that is good?"

The Baroness smiled. "My dear, you make too much of this. I am certain Lord Beaumont searches his mind this very instant for a suitable comparison to your hair."

Juliana said, "But Sir Richard does not need to search his mind. This morning he said my hair was the sun and my eyes like twilight."

The Baroness waved her hands. "It is all well and good for Sir Richard to have his wits about him and pay pretty compliments. His future is not at stake here. I can assure you that when Sir Richard thinks of marrying he shall be significantly more tongue-tied."

Juliana seemed uncertain.

"Trust me, my dear. The more awkward Beaumont acts, the more struck he is with you. There is quite a difference between flirtation and real feeling. And do not forget that he is an earl, while Sir Richard is merely a knight. You cannot expect an earl to be as frivolous."

Juliana shrugged. "One could expect he could say something clever. But, as you say, perhaps he is tongue-tied."

Madeleine inwardly groaned. She had thought Lord Beaumont would do the work himself. Now she saw she would indeed have to help him along. Although in an entirely different direction than her mother was planning.

Agnes stumbled into the room. She dropped slightly, in the barest of curtsies. "M'lady, your nephew be here. I showed him to the great hall. He be with that other gentleman. The rude one."

Chapter Six – A Cousin Arrives

The Baroness said, "Agnes, kindly keep your opinions to yourself. Provide my cousin and Lord Beaumont with refreshment. I shall be down directly."

Agnes stomped from the room muttering, "But he is rude. Anybody can see it."

Juliana said, "I am not up to greeting my cousin just yet. I have had a trying morning and must look a fright. I shall rest and join you later."

"Quite right, my dear," the Baroness said to Juliana. "Give Beaumont time to miss you. Excellent thought."

"And I, also, shall join you later," Madeleine said. "I am determined to finish this sewing."

The Baroness smiled. "You have never been determined to finish your sewing."

Madeleine reddened. "True. But today I feel determined as I have never felt before. Except perhaps on Alfred's last visit."

"You shall come with me and greet your cousin," the Baroness said. "You must not expect the Alfred you remember. He may be greatly changed."

Madeleine threw down her mangled embroidery. "One can only pray," she muttered.

Madeleine followed her mother out of the bower. Before they had even neared the great hall, Alfred's over-loud voice ricocheted down the passageway.

"M'lord, when the subject is hawking, there can be no better person to consult than I. Show me a good Norwegian falcon and I shall right her smallest difficulties."

Madeleine heard Beaumont's low voice, say, "A comfort to know."

Madeleine's face burned already and they had not even reached the hall. She wanted to turn and run. Run from jeering Beaumont, from ridiculous Alfred. Run from the castle and into the forest where the only beings that could note her shame were the deer and rabbits.

But they had arrived in the great hall.

The two gentlemen bowed. Madeleine and the Baroness dropped into curtsies. Before they had time to rise, Alfred had bounded across the room. His balding head bounced with each step as if, had he walked any faster, it might take flight from his shoulders.

Alfred grasped the Baroness' hand and jerked her up from her curtsy. "Dear Aunt, has it been two years? You look as girlish as ever."

Beaumont stood behind Alfred, his arms folded, with a small smile on his lips.

Alfred turned to Madeleine. "And you, dear cousin, have grown into a woman."

"The Baroness has become a girl and her daughter a woman. Most extraordinary," the earl said.

Alfred blinked.

The Baroness seemed momentarily confused. She gathered herself. "I am delighted to see you, Alfred. As is Madeleine."

Beaumont looked at Madeleine with an inquiring glance. She thought she would blush further if that had been possible. But she already felt as if her cheeks were the color of claret.

"My father sends his apologies," Alfred said. "As you know, he is an important and busy man."

"We are sorry not to see him," the Baroness said. "Though it is a happy circumstance that my brother sends you in his place."

"Happy indeed, M'lady," Alfred said. "My father, though a great man, is not the hunter I am. I find our Lord Beaumont keen on the sport. It is truly a piece of luck that I am here to advise him."

Beaumont cleared his throat. "Yes, indeed. Your cousin has already shared much of his mind with me. Though we have been acquainted so briefly."

Alfred walked to Beaumont and slapped him on the back. As Beaumont recovered from the surprise assault, Alfred said, "Fear not, friend. By the end of your visit you shall be as expert as I with the noble falcon."

"Perhaps I've not the innate talent you appear to have been blessed with," the earl said drily.

"Nonsense, M'lord. I shall bring you along at a good pace. We may even bring a longbow and try our luck that way. I am an excellent shot."

Alfred turned away from Beaumont and stared Madeleine full in the face. One of his small brown eyes winked at her. "Naturally, cousin, you shall want to accompany us and observe our prowess."

Madeleine thought she would rather sink her hands into boiling water than witness her cousin's absurdity. She knew very well that Alfred offended the earl with his own peculiar brand of pomposity and condescension. Beaumont would play with Alfred and sneer at him and Alfred would never note it.

She hated them both. Alfred for his stupidity and Beaumont for his perception of it. She had a great, and thoroughly un-ladylike, urge to seize Alfred's round, balding head and break a glazed window with it.

Instead, Madeleine smiled. "It would be a great pleasure. Were I not ill."

Beaumont stepped forward. "You are unwell? Do you require a Physician? I shall ride this instant..."

Madeleine was startled. "No, certainly not. It is just a headache. Rest and quiet are all I require."

The Baroness stared at Madeleine, but said nothing.

Sir Richard and Juliana entered the hall. Juliana patted Sir Richard's arm. "Simply shameless, Sir."

Juliana sank into a curtsy and Sir Richard bowed. "Hello, cousin," Juliana said.

The Baroness pressed her lips together. "I thought you rested in the bower, Juliana."

Juliana colored. "I did. I was. But Sir Richard sent Agnes to rouse me. He thought it a poor thing that I not greet my cousin on his arrival."

Sir Richard bowed. "Only a poor thing for your cousin."

The Baroness narrowed her eyes at Sir Richard.

Alfred said, "You look well, Juliana, as always. Though I cannot note the sort of improvement I have seen in Madeleine."

The great hall sunk into silence.

"Naturally, I've a particular interest in Madeleine's progress," Alfred said.

Madeleine wanted to disappear into one of the tapestries hung on the walls. Perhaps she could hide behind a stag, never to be seen again.

"Ah, but that is a private conversation, is it not?" Alfred continued.

Beaumont stepped forward. "Sir" the earl said to Alfred. "Perhaps you would condescend to show Sir Richard and me this remarkable falcon of yours."

Madeleine felt a surge of gratitude, though she could not imagine Beaumont had diverted Alfred to save her any pain.

"Naturally, M'lord, delighted," Alfred said. "It is only unfortunate that the day is too advanced for a hunt. After you have seen my noble bird, you shall insist on being out at first light on the morrow."

Beaumont said, "No doubt."

Madeleine, her legs feeling as if they might give out from under her, really did feel ill now. She bobbled a curtsy, mumbled, "excuse me," and fled the room.

Madeleine stumbled into the bower and flung herself on the bed. Her mother had been much mistaken. Alfred was the same bombastic fool he had been two years before. What had he thought of? Singling her out and making reference to a private conversation? As if the betrothal were happily arranged and agreed on? As if she would welcome such a proposal.

Madeleine felt a sudden sinking feeling. Perhaps it had been happily arranged and agreed on. She knew her mother and her uncle wished it, yet she had never envisioned this day would arrive. Had she not said she would enter a convent rather than marry that jester? Was that not enough to indicate her abhorrence of the idea?

She rolled over and buried her face into the linen-covered pillow. A small, bitter laugh escaped her. The Baroness and her uncle had not concerned themselves with Madeleine's feelings on the matter. They would have her marry Alfred against her will. Alfred had been sent on this visit to propose.

Madeleine sat up and said aloud, "I will not do it. They cannot force me." Her head did really pound now and she sank back down. Her eyes closed and she heard the rustle of a gown. Her mother said, "Madeleine, are you truly ill?"

Madeleine opened her eyes as her mother sat on the side of the bed, arranging her gown. She said, "I am ill as only Alfred can make me. He is a walking plague in every sense."

"Tsk, Madeleine, you speak as if you were the heiress of a large fortune. As if you could pick and choose as you like. You are old enough now to grasp the realities of our situation."

Madeleine sat up. "Why him? I know I must make a creditable marriage someday, but it need not be Alfred."

"It need not be Alfred? Who need it be then?" The Baroness heaved a sigh. "We have no silver to rent a house in Bellham for the season, nor buy piles of pretty gowns, nor throw grand dinner parties and balls. We have not the means to present you to society."

"Then why does not Juliana marry Alfred?"

"You know perfectly well why."

Madeleine sat in silence, wondering if her mother would actually say it.

The Baroness said, "Madeleine, I ask you to face the facts. Juliana does not need to be shown off in Bellham or have an array of gowns. Her beauty is known far and wide. It was only a matter of time before an eligible suitor would present himself."

"Ah," Madeleine said, "but I am not known far and wide. I would need be swathed in yards of velvet and drag a heavy dowry behind me to have anything like a choice."

The Baroness patted Madeleine's hand. "You are not ill-looking, my dear, as you well know. I've no doubt any man long in your company would describe you as pretty. It is just that you do not have Juliana's classical beauty. Her looks are much admired and sought after. Yours are...more original."

Madeleine didn't speak.

Her mother fidgeted with her gown. "Be sensible. Your future security is at stake. Think you the Baron de Clare was my choice? I was young once; I had my girlish dreams. There was even a young knight…oh never mind. The point is, I had to be sensible."

"You did not choose my father?"

"Of course not. He was chosen for me." She stroked Madeleine's hair. "It was all for the best. I became a Baroness and, over time, I grew fond of him. He could be very amusing, you know. It is not only your hair that reminds me of him. You have his peculiar wit."

"Mother, I shall never grow fond of Alfred. Because he shall always be Alfred. And I think there must be some law against cousins marrying. I am sure it is so."

"Yes, well, happily there is no law against marrying a cousin who is only a cousin by marriage." The Baroness looked away and said softly, "I shall always wonder at my brother marrying that woman. Still, they've done well together and your uncle has raised Alfred as his own son." The Baroness turned and looked into Madeleine's eyes. "Do not you see it, my dear? Marry Alfred and much is accomplished. With your uncle's money, de Clare castle shall be returned to what it was."

"Mother, I understand perfectly well why you wish this. But what of Alfred? He's rich. He can marry who he likes. He can marry someone who likes him. And if Juliana does indeed marry the earl, let him repair our finances."

"It is not only about money, Madeleine. It is my brother's particular wish that you marry because while Alfred might marry a girl he likes, it would not be a Baron's daughter. Alfred's parentage on his mother's side is a bit…low. Marrying you would secure Alfred's station in life."

The Baroness rose and shook out the folds of her gown. "You must be practical, for all our sakes. Marry Alfred, and mold him into something tolerable. You shall find a way to get along with him. The world is not a perfect place, but we must all work within its confines."

The Baroness walked toward the door, then paused and said over her shoulder, "And pray do not threaten the convent again. I would sooner believe the earth round."

Madeleine spent the rest of the afternoon in the bower. She had no wish to see anyone. She thought she might spend the rest of her life there, only near the supper hour her stomach began to rumble.

She debated whether she might creep to the kitchen unnoticed. There would be nothing she'd like better than a quiet dinner in Godfrey's company. Madeleine would not even care if he were drunk. Even in Godfrey's worst state he could not be as offensive as Beaumont and Alfred.

With a sigh Madeleine rolled off the bed and straightened her hair. She knew her mother's eyes would be sharper than Alfred's falcon when it came to her whereabouts this night.

"So," she said, in a quiet voice, "I go to the great hall and face the beasts, each with his own particular poison." Madeleine peered into the looking glass. "I shall not marry Alfred and I do not care what the mighty Beaumont thinks of us."

She felt slightly cheered as she left the bower.

The others were already gathered in the great hall. A fire burned in the massive stone hearth. A tray of silver goblets and a jug of wine sat on the table in front of the Baroness.

Alfred had his cup in his hand and leaned over the Baroness. "Excellent wine, Aunt. My discerning palate tells me it comes from the southeast of Baden. Tell me it is so."

The Baroness, looking slightly annoyed, said, "Truly Alfred, as I said a moment ago, I know not. It is from the Baron's cellar."

Beaumont sat across from the Baroness with his usual small smile.

Sir Richard and Juliana stood talking near one of the glazed windows. Madeleine glanced down at her old gown. She thought Juliana had never looked better.

As they perceived her entrance, Beaumont rose and the men bowed. The earl walked over to her. "Are you well?"

Madeleine curtsied. "Quite recovered, thank you."

Alfred elbowed in front of the earl. "I am privileged to know something of the healing arts, Lord Beaumont. Note the flush in her cheeks. To an untrained eye an erroneous diagnosis of fever might be perceived. But the discerning eye sees the flush does not proceed to the forehead. A clear indication of good health."

Beaumont bowed. "I defer to your superior knowledge."

Alfred puffed himself up. "It is a quality of good breeding and thorough education to be always curious about areas one has not been acquainted with."

"Curious indeed," Beaumont said.

Alfred turned to Madeleine. "You may rely on many happy days in future acquiring such knowledge." He looked over his shoulder to the earl. "I am not one of those men, Lord, who hoards knowledge. Not even from the weaker sex."

Beaumont said, "Nobody who had the pleasure of your company would ever think it of you."

"Thank you. It has always been my wish to better the understanding of those not fortunate enough to have my sort of education," Alfred said, smoothing his bald head. "I deplore the man who does not feel as I do."

The Baroness glanced at the dining table with a look of desperation. She jumped up. "Well, I believe supper is ready." She held her arm out to Beaumont.

"I would not deprive your nephew of the pleasure of escorting you on his first night," the earl said. He turned to Madeleine and held his arm out.

Madeleine was startled. She took the earl's arm. Alfred and her mother preceded them. Under Alfred's booming voice, Beaumont said, "Is it true you are to marry your cousin?"

Madeleine wanted to scream that she would never marry such a colossal oaf. But she found herself too angry with Beaumont to even hint at the truth. She said, "That can be of no concern to you, M'lord. He may not be an earl, but his respectability cannot be questioned."

Beaumont looked at her with a puzzled expression.

Sir Richard and Juliana had finally realized it was time to sit for supper and came up behind. The Baroness sat at the head of the table and Madeleine found herself between Alfred and Beaumont. She thought it would have been better to have starved in the bower, then have found herself thus seated.

The only bright spot was the table. Godfrey was nowhere in sight. The shining nef boxes were in place and each plate had a round, baked trencher.

The earl sliced meat from their shared plate and placed it on her trencher. Madeleine thanked the heavens. If Godfrey had been drinking, it was blessedly little. The supper would be forgettable, Godfrey's usually were. But it appeared entirely respectable.

Madeleine looked across the table to Juliana and Sir Richard. Both were in high spirits, laughing and talking as if there were no one else in the room. Why did not Juliana engage the earl in conversation? How could she be so selfish as to leave Madeleine stuck with him?

The Baroness glanced at Juliana as if she wondered the same thing, but she was quickly overpowered by Alfred's remarks and questions. He nearly shouted, "I would know my father's beef anywhere. I am correct?"

The Baroness sighed. "Yes, it is the beef my brother sent with you."

Madeleine, feeling decent manners required her to say something to her supper partner, said, "M'lord, do you indeed enjoy hunting?"

"With the right company, nearly anything is enjoyable," the earl said.

Madeleine understood his meaning. Beaumont might like hunting, but did not expect to like it on the morrow with Alfred. She had grown tired of his unending barbs, whether justified or not.

She said, "Of course, even the most enjoyable activity, such as supper, may be ruined by the wrong company."

The earl smiled. "We cannot always have our relations conduct themselves as we would wish."

Madeleine stared straight ahead. "I do not refer to my relations."

She peeked out of the corner of her eye. To her satisfaction, she saw the look of confusion on the earl's face. Then the flush when he understood her meaning.

He stammered, "I did not mean...I would not offend..."

Madeleine felt herself suddenly growing very cheerful. "I perceived your meaning perfectly, as you perceived mine."

The earl paled.

They spent the remainder of the supper staring straight ahead.

Alfred heralded the end of the meal with the spirited cry, "Sirs, we ride at dawn! Let the forest and its prey beware our assault."

Chapter Seven – Red-Headed, Sadly

In the bower, Agnes struggled to part the Baroness from her gown. Juliana stared at her reflection in the dark panes of glaze in the window.

"Ouch," cried the Baroness. "Can you not undress me without killing me?"

Agnes muttered, "'Twould not kill the lady to say a kind word now and again."

Madeleine sat on the edge of the bed. Her mind raced in all directions. She felt a great need for Godfrey's counsel. She said, "Mother, shall I go to the kitchens to plan the morrow's meals?"

The Baroness waved her hand distractedly. "Yes, do."

Madeleine hurried to the passageway before her mother changed her mind. She guessed the men were still in the great hall in front of the fire. She would take the servant's door; she could not bear to see her cousin or Beaumont again this night.

Their voices drifted from the hall. She drew closer as Beaumont said, "Are you formally engaged, then?"

Madeleine paused. She knew she should not stay and listen. As she had discovered, it was all too easy to hear things one would rather not. She firmly determined to go. Yet her feet would not move.

"Nearly so," Alfred said. "My father and aunt have agreed on it."

"And you have ascertained the lady's feelings?" Beaumont asked.

Madeleine cringed at Alfred's booming laugh.

"Madeleine's feelings?" he said. "What could they be but approving?"

There was a silence, then Alfred said, "Certainly, M'lord, you have noticed her blushes in my presence."

Beaumont's tone was thoughtful. "I have indeed."

"Some men would flinch at the hair. Red, sadly," Alfred said. "But I can overlook such a trifle."

Madeleine gasped. She slapped a hand over her mouth.

Sir Richard said, "Madeleine's coloring is very pretty." He sighed and said softly, "But I am cursed to love sun-kissed wheat."

Madeleine willed herself to move and hurried away. She ran across the yard. Red, sadly? Overlook such a trifle? What generosity of spirit her cousin had! She supposed she must be equally generous and overlook that Alfred's own hair color was but a memory. Overlook, indeed.

By the time Madeleine burst into the kitchen she felt that were she a man, she would thrash Alfred.

Godfrey sat by the fire with an earthenware jug in his hand. He looked up, startled, and cried, "Don't you go a-yellin'. This be me first drop all day."

Madeleine collapsed into the chair next to him. "Drink away. Your love of ale is the least of my concerns."

Godfrey set down his cup. "A startlin' statement."

Madeleine put her head in her hands. "It's all so awful."

Godfrey patted her shoulder. "There, girl. This ain't like you. Tell me the whole of it."

Madeleine took a deep breath. "My mother and uncle have conspired to get Alfred here to offer for my hand. My mother says he's my only hope for a husband. Beaumont has amused himself at everyone's expense all day, and I was rude to him at supper. Oh, and I believe Sir Richard is in love with Juliana."

Godfrey let out a low whistle. "That be a lot to chew on. All right. First Alfred. What will you do about him?"

"I know not! I cannot marry him. Yet, how can I refuse? My only threat is to enter a convent and my mother knows I will never do it."

Godfrey took a long swig of ale. "As for Alfred bein' your only chance at a husband, I don't give that no credence. And if your sister marries Beaumont, we got silver and nobody needs Alfred."

"But I am trying to prevent Juliana from marrying Beaumont. Remember?"

"Aye. I remember. But if one of you need be sacrificed, let it be Juliana."

Madeleine colored. She was ashamed she had thought the same thing. She said, "Were it that easy."

"Don't see nothing hard about it."

"Godfrey, if I marry Alfred, I shall be miserable. If Juliana marries Beaumont, she shall be miserable and I shall be miserable knowing I let her do it to spare myself."

Godfrey snorted. "M'lady, try turnin' that one round. If you marry Alfred, will your sister be miserable for you?"

"No, I think not..."

"Mark me, I'm right. Don't go throwin' your life away over a girl what's never given you half a thought."

Godfrey's words stung. Because they were true. Juliana would not give Madeleine's happiness half a thought. She never had. Why shouldn't Madeleine allow Juliana to marry Beaumont? Would it not be exactly what she deserved? And if the silver were no longer a concern, if it were only Alfred's station in life to consider, might not her mother be pressed to relent?

Madeleine sighed. "It is tempting. Very tempting. But I cannot."

"Why ever not, you barmy lass?"

Madeleine tried to find the words to say what she knew to be true. "Juliana may not be as we would wish. But she is not mean-spirited."

Godfrey looked annoyed. "So that be her excuse?"

Madeleine stared down at her hands, twisting them together. "Remember last summer, when you served a fish stew and she remarked that the salt cellar is meant to be used sparingly?"

Godfrey nodded, smiling.

"And you said, the world would thank her for sharing her opinions more sparingly?"

"That deflated her sails quick enough."

"She cried until she was sick from it."

Godfrey's head snapped up. "What?"

"It took hours to get her over it. Oh, she railed against you. Wanted you thrown out that very night. But, truly, it was that her feelings were hurt."

Godfrey leaned back and crossed his arms.

"It is always like that with Juliana. She is easily stung, yet never thinks of others. She is ridiculous, I know. She should give others the same consideration she gives herself. But she cannot."

Godfrey sat in silence, his arms still crossed. Madeleine thought he looked unimpressed.

"Godfrey, she would not survive Beaumont's tongue. She would die of grief." Madeleine paused, then said softly, "But I am made of sterner stuff."

Godfrey chewed on his lip. "So you gonna marry that ninny?"

"Not if I can think of a way out that does not involve Juliana marrying Beaumont."

"Why cannot she marry Sir Richard? He seems willin.' Don't he got nothin' to offer?"

"I believe not. He is a knight; they are generally poor."

Godfrey nodded.

Madeleine said, "For the morrow, I shall endeavor to prevent Alfred catching me alone. Though it shall not be easy. My mother has a way of contriving these things."

Godfrey leaned back in his chair. "Would that your father still lived. That man knew how to run an estate. We should never have come to such a pass."

"But he is not here," Madeleine said. "And you, my dear, are my only advisor."

Godfrey drained his ale jug. "God save us all."

Chapter Eight – The Arrow Hits its Mark

The following morning, Madeleine heard the stomp of hooves and the snorts of impatient horses drifting up from the yard. The men were leaving for the hunt. She went down the stairs to break her fast, thankful she would at least have that meal in peace.

Though her mother and Juliana were already seated, the table in the great hall was quiet. The Baroness busied herself with a plate of cold meat. Juliana stared over Madeleine's head.

They spent the best part of an hour in silence. Madeleine itched for her mother to rise and excuse them. She wanted to be up and away from the oppressive hall.

The Baroness put down her knife. "Madeleine, you will show Alfred the estate this afternoon."

Madeleine felt her spirits sink. It was well and good to talk of evading Alfred. But how might she do it?

The Baroness turned to Juliana. "And you, my dear, shall attend to your sewing here in the hall. I shall see to it that Sir Richard is gotten out of the way."

Juliana shook herself out of her daze. "What of Sir Richard?"

"I shall find him employment. Some errand."

"What errand?"

"I do not know. What can it matter? It shall provide Lord Beaumont with an opportunity."

Juliana played with her ale cup. "Oh. Beaumont."

"Of course, Beaumont. Good heavens, girl, what ails---"

Before the Baroness could finish, the double doors to the great hall crashed open. Alfred's falconer stumbled in. He was red-faced and out of breath.

The Baroness jumped up. "What is it? Speak, man!"

The falconer held a stitch in his side. He choked out, "Terrible accident. I fear he is killed."

The Baroness steadied herself against the edge of the table. "Alfred. Dear Lord, my brother will never forgive me."

Juliana cried, "Richard!"

Madeleine sat staring ahead. Could it be true? Could Alfred be dead?"

The clattering of hooves in the yard broke the silence. Juliana ran from the table, with the Baroness and Madeleine at her heels.

Before Madeleine caught sight of the yard, she heard Juliana cry, "Thank the saints!"

So it was not Sir Richard. Had it then been Alfred? She felt her cheeks flame as she realized how much she wished it. To be released from him through no fault of her own!

She burst out the doors and into the yard. Alfred sat on his horse, very much alive. He stared straight ahead as if he were in a trance.

Sir Richard carried Lord Beaumont, limp in his arms, an arrow protruding from his chest.

Madeleine drew in a breath. Beaumont! He had been killed. She felt as if the air had thinned and she could not get enough into her chest.

Through her muddled thinking Madeleine saw her mother and sister running in circles, seeming to have no destination in mind.

Sir Richard's commanding voice broke through Madeleine's haze. "We must get him to bed. I shall ride for the physician!"

Madeleine shook her head, trying to clear her mind. Physician? Is the earl not dead, could he be—

Sir Richard strode past her, Beaumont draped in his arms. "Please. Help me get him inside."

Madeleine was finally shaken to action. She hurried into the castle, throwing doors open in front of Sir Richard.

Agnes stood, slack-jawed, in the hall.

Madeleine shouted, "Tell Godfrey we have need of him. And bring me the medicinals chest." Agnes stood as if she were a statue. "Quickly!"

They raced down a corridor to the bedchamber Lord Beaumont occupied. Madeleine threw open the door. Sir Richard gently laid his friend on the bed.

Beaumont's skin had turned from its usual sun-burnished brown to ashen. His breathing came shallow and slow. The arrow in his chest pointed to the rafters, its tail feathers looking as if they might take flight.

Madeleine had been so eager to rid the castle of the earl. Now that he lay dying she felt a wave of regret. He had an unpleasant manner. What of that? There were far worse sins. And he had been Sir Richard's loyal friend. Beaumont had not deserved this.

Sir Richard paced the room and ran a hand through his hair. "Where lives the nearest physician?"

In a quiet voice, Madeleine said, "John of Barchester is just three miles from the castle. But I know him to be in Bellham for at least a fortnight."

"Surely, there is another. A barber, at least?"

"Ben Gundon. He is in the town of Minster. It is a day's ride."

"And the Baroness?" Sir Richard asked. "Is she skilled?"

"My mother and Juliana have no affinity for the healing arts. Godfrey's wife Bertha tended the sick and injured. She taught me as much as she could before she died." Madeleine paused. "I hope it was enough."

"It must be," Sir Richard said. "At least until I return. I shall go at once. I will fetch physician Gundon and ride all night. We shall arrive by dawn on the morrow."

Madeleine was not certain if Sir Richard did not fully comprehend, or if he chose not to. "The arrow cannot remain in place as long as that. It shall bring on a fever."

Sir Richard clenched and unclenched his hands, but said nothing.

"If we are to remove it, it would be kinder to do so while he sleeps." Madeleine said quietly.

Sir Richard looked at the arrow, then at Madeleine. He said, "We cannot pull it out. We would have to push it through. We might...it could..."

Madeleine felt her stomach turn over. "Yes. Only a skilled surgeon would know which organs might be struck. We can but guess. But it will surely kill him to leave it thus for four and twenty hours."

Sir Richard struck the heavy oak mantel above the hearth. "I would gladly murder your cousin."

"Alfred?" Madeleine asked, startled.

Sir Richard let out a small and bitter laugh. "You cannot think my aim that bad."

Madeleine sank into the chair at the writing desk. "Alfred has done this?"

"He has indeed," Sir Richard said. "Had I an idea his arrow was well-aimed, I would cut out his heart."

"But, you do not think..."

"No. I do not. He aimed at I know not what. A rustle in the grass. He released too soon."

The Baroness and Juliana poked their heads through the doorway. Juliana looked at Sir Richard. The Baroness stared at Beaumont. She gripped the doorframe. "God save us."

Juliana seemed shaken out of her reverie by her mother's voice. She glanced at the bed and cried, "Ugh!"

Madeleine hurried over. She backed them away from the door. "Wait down in the hall. You can do nothing here."

They both seemed much relieved and turned on their heels.

Madeleine shut the door. "What will you do to Alfred?"

Sir Richard's face twisted in anger. "Nothing. Yet. It shall be for my friend to decide. If he lives." He turned away from the bed. "If he does not..."

Godfrey threw open the door. He carried a pitcher of steaming water in one hand and clean linen in the other. He stopped short. "By the saints, 'tis true. Your shandy cousin has killed an earl."

Madeleine said, "He is not dead, praise God. But we must remove the arrow."

"Remove it?" Godfrey asked. "But Barchester's gone to Bellham."

"I know. We shall need your help."

Madeleine felt strangely calm as she directed Godfrey and Sir Richard to tear the linen into bandaging strips. She refused to let her mind drift to what they were about to do. She had only done it once before. And really, she had not done it at all. Bertha had. The man had died two days later.

Agnes stumbled in with the medicinals chest. Madeleine grabbed it from her hands and pushed the babbling maid out of the room. She sat the leather chest on her lap and opened the lid. She found the jar she was looking for. She untied the string that held the parchment covering in place. The mixed aromas of honey, fox clote and yarrow drifted into the room. It had been specially mixed to prevent infection, and the fever that would come with it. She would mix a draught for pain when it was needed. If it were needed.

Madeleine glanced at Beaumont and her breath caught. He was himself, yet he was not. With no sneer to mar his features, no stinging words on his tongue, he appeared transformed.

His face was as it had ever been - the straight, proud nose, high cheekbones and strong chin. But a blond curl had fallen on his forehead and the dusky lashes that framed his closed eyes gave him a gentle aspect Madeleine would not have thought possible.

Sir Richard interrupted her thoughts. "I believe we are ready. If we hold him up, can you..."

Madeleine understood his meaning. She must push the arrow deeper into Beaumont's chest. She dreaded doing it. She didn't see how she could do it. But it must be done and she had not the strength to hold him steady while someone else did it.

Sir Richard snapped off the feathered end of the arrow. He used his knife to cut off Beaumont's surcoat.

Sir Richard and Godfrey grasped Beaumont's limp body and pulled him upright.

Godfrey said, "Come, gal. Be your father's daughter. Firm and steady-like. Don't hesitate."

Madeleine grasped the shaft of the arrow.

Sir Richard said, "We do the right thing, do we not?"

In a shaking voice, Madeleine said, "I believe so. The arrow is not near the heart. If we have luck, we shall miss the lung as well."

Sir Richard murmured, "Luck..."

Godfrey said, "No time to waste. He may well wake while we be jawin' about it."

Madeleine tightened her grip on the shaft and pushed. Despite Godfrey's warning not to hesitate, when she felt the arrow plunge through tissue, she did hesitate. Beaumont groaned.

Godfrey said, "No turnin' back. Get it done."

Madeleine wanted to run from the room. But the thought of Beaumont waking with the arrow half way through his chest was too much to bear.

She bit her lip and pushed. The shaft suddenly gave in her hand.

Godfrey said, "You be through. Come round the back of him and pull it out."

Madeleine scrambled around Godfrey to Beaumont's back. It was broad and muscular, the only blemish being the bloodied arrowhead piercing the skin below his right shoulder.

She grasped it and pulled. Now that the arrowhead was clear, the rest of the shaft slid through easily. Before she knew it, the arrow was free. She dropped it and it clattered on the floor. A river of blood ran down Beaumont's back and turned the bed linen crimson.

"The bandages," Madeleine cried, "before he bleeds to death." She grabbed a piece of the linen she had soaked in the honey salve and held it against the wound. Godfrey used all his might to hold Beaumont up while Sir Richard did the same to the wound on his chest. She and Sir Richard wrapped strips of linen to hold the bandages in place. Once the bandages were secure, Madeleine directed Godfrey to lay Beaumont on his side.

Madeleine carefully washed the blood from his back. She felt awkward doing it. She had cleaned the wounds of any number of villagers. And in some places not fit to be discussed in polite company. She was not shy or overly modest. But they had been cowherds and farmers. Not earls. Not this particular earl.

Between the three of them, with much shifting and grunting, they got the bed linen changed.

Madeleine sank into a chair and wiped the sweat from her face.

Godfrey patted her shoulder. "Well done."

Madeleine looked at Beaumont. His eyes were still closed and his breathing remained shallow. "Perhaps. But he does not wake."

"Give him time. He has had a shock, and lost a deal a' blood besides. For now, it be a blessing he sleeps."

Sir Richard said, "I ride for the physician this instant. I shall not rest until I am returned."

"You go on, Sir," Godfrey said. "The two of us be lookin' after your friend."

Sir Richard fingered his sword. "Pray God I do not see your cousin before I go."

Madeleine understood him. Sir Richard did not wish to do anything he might regret. Though Madeleine did not think she would regret anything Sir Richard might care to do to her idiot cousin.

Godfrey said, "Alfred be a daft soul, but most careful of his own person. I expect he be hidin' in a cupboard somewhere."

Sir Richard put his hand on Godfrey's shoulder. "You are a good man. I count on you to help until I return. I know all in the castle shall want to assist, but it is you and Madeleine I must pin my hopes on."

After Sir Richard left, Madeleine measured out comfrey, laurel and white willow bark. Godfrey took them to the kitchen to prepare a draught for pain and fever.

Madeleine sat for a while, staring at Beaumont. He occasionally grimaced and moaned, but did not wake.

She stood and paced the room. Her thoughts raced ahead of her. Alfred! How could he have done it? How had he been so careless? Despite wishing to believe it merely an accident that might have befallen anyone, she could imagine the course of events.

Alfred had tried to impress, with no skills to impress with. He had nearly killed a man, and may yet have done, in the pursuit of his own self-importance.

And that buffoon was the man she was meant to marry?

Madeleine colored as she thought of Beaumont's barbs at her family. He should not have said them. Out of common courtesy, he should not. But that did not make them untrue.

No longer able to think on the events of the morning, and her family's part in it, Madeleine sank back into the chair. She rested her elbow on the desk and felt something slide underneath it. Her elbow had pushed forward a piece of parchment.

It was covered in a close, fine hand. Of course, she thought, he would have a fine hand.

Madeleine had no intention of reading the letter. She would not for the world pry into another's private affairs. And yet, her eyes insisted on drifting in that direction.

She thought to lay the extra linen over the parchment, so as not to be tempted. Then, she muttered, "I am a disgrace," leaned over the desk and read it.

Dearest Father,

I write from de Clare castle. At our last meeting you were so kind as to inform me of your wishes regarding my future. I have, in good faith, met both Caroline de Quincy and Juliana de Clare. It pains me to inform you that neither is suitable. The de Quincy girl is a stout and giggling lump. She would hardly be welcomed by my dear mother. Juliana de Clare is passably pretty, but lacks the fine mind and judgment we wish for.

Before you grow angry with me, there is one who might please you, as she has pleased me. The younger de Clare daughter. I write for your approval of this alliance.

Madeleine caught her breath. What was this? What did he mean? She was the younger de Clare daughter.

The rest of the letter was still covered in sand, but Madeleine had no scruples now. She hastily shook it off.

I continue this letter after supper. I had a great urge to throw it into the fire and begin again, but it is well you know all. I had thought I would pursue the younger daughter, Madeleine. Her cousin fancies they are engaged, but as no formal announcement had been made, I did not countenance it. However, the Lady made her feelings known this evening. I am not to her liking.

I shall quit de Clare castle as soon as I can decently make my excuses. Please assure my mother and sister I have not forgotten them. Sir Richard and I shall travel to Bellham to carry out their errands before returning home.

It pains me that I do not send the joyous news you seek.

Faithfully,

Henry

Madeleine dropped the parchment.

Chapter Nine – Lord Beaumont's Letter

Madeleine sat stunned. How had this happened? Beaumont had planned to ask for her hand?

She grabbed the parchment from the floor and read it again.

There was no mistake. Beaumont had thought to marry her. And she had made short work of it.

"Well," she said aloud, "excellent. I would not have married him for the world."

She looked at his face, pale and defenseless. "What a horrible, proud man."

Madeleine repeated this idea to herself in an effort to calm her runaway thoughts. And yet, she did not feel as convinced as she would have liked. Other, different, thoughts had begun to creep in.

Exactly what had been so horrible about him? Certainly not his appearance. Yes, he had been proud. And he had a tongue as sharp as a butcher's knife. Did not Madeleine have a sharp tongue on occasion? And had he not had the discernment to recognize her good qualities?

It pained her to think of herself in Beaumont's place. Had she been the visitor to such a household, what remarks might she have made?

Madeleine doubted she would have said them aloud, as he had. But she did not doubt their thoughts ran alike.

It did not signify now. Even if Madeleine had not driven him off with her sharp words, it did not signify. Beaumont might not recover from his injury. And if he did, the earl could have no intention of joining himself to the family of his near murderer.

A groan startled her from her thoughts. Beaumont blinked slightly, then was still again.

Madeleine realized she still had the parchment in her hand. She threw it down on the desk. She brushed up the sand that had scattered in all directions and dusted it over the second half of the letter as it had been. She felt like a criminal.

Beaumont groaned. He whispered, "Do not..."

Madeleine rushed to the bedstead.

Beaumont opened his eyes. He looked at Madeleine in confusion. He tried to sit up, winced and looked down at the bandages across his chest. In a rasping voice, he said, "I bid the fool not to shoot."

"Do not speak," Madeleine said. "You have been gravely wounded."

The earl ignored her. He craned his neck and searched the room. "Where is Richard?"

"He has gone to fetch the physician," Madeleine said. "He shall return on the morrow."

Beaumont sank back down. "Good Lord. Has not a physician tended me? The arrow was in my chest."

"Yes. Well. It is no longer," Madeleine said.

Beaumont looked at her thoughtfully. "Did you--"

"Yes," Madeleine said quietly. "Now, you should rest."

Beaumont shifted on the pallet and groaned. In a weak voice he said, "I believe I must. Your cousin's speeches were painful enough. But this is extraordinary."

Godfrey opened the door. "Ah. He is awake." He set down a pitcher and goblet. "I have the draught. We best get it in him."

Beaumont eyed the pitcher. "What now? Poison?"

Godfrey laughed. "No, M'lord. Alfred had no hand in this. I cooked it up meself."

"I have tasted your cooking," Beaumont croaked.

Madeleine said, "The draught shall help you sleep."

"Your cousin would have me sleep eternal," Beaumont muttered.

Godfrey reached around the earl's shoulders and propped him up. Madeleine filled the goblet and held it to his lips. He took a small sip and choked. "It is indeed poison."

"You must drink," Madeleine said firmly.

Beaumont, with much struggle and complaint, drained the cup.

Godfrey laid him back down. The earl closed his eyes. After some minutes, his breathing became regular and deep.

"He sleeps," Madeleine said.

Godfrey sat down in the chair across from Madeleine. He stretched his legs out in front of him. "You be right about him. He is rudeness his self."

"I can hear you," Beaumont whispered.

Godfrey jumped up. "Well, now. I best get back to the kitchens. The household is in an uproar." He hurried from the room.

To Madeleine's relief, the draught finally took effect and the earl did really sleep. She needed some quiet with no distractions. She had much to consider.

She thought of what it would mean to marry Beaumont. To marry...Henry. Of course, he was horrible. She would not give up that opinion. But then, he was pleasing to look at. And he was not Alfred. Alfred was both horrible and horrible to look at. And if she did marry the earl, would not that save Juliana from him better than anything could?

It pleased Madeleine to think of sacrificing herself in that manner. She brushed aside the thought that it had not pleased her when the object was Alfred.

It also cheered her to think that Madeleine could be the instrument of the castle's restoration. The silver would come from her pockets. Her mother would have to acknowledge that. And then Juliana might marry any poor knight she liked.

Yes, Madeleine thought, it would suit on all accounts. As for her own suffering in the matter, as her mother had said of Alfred, she might mold Beaumont into something tolerable.

Madeleine decided that if Beaumont should ask, she would have no thought of her own happiness. She would accept.

Then Madeleine remembered she had already put an end to the earl's plans. He would not ask.

She would have to help him on. To somehow indicate that, despite how she had treated him so far, he should ask. That as odious as Madeleine would regard it, she would accept. For her family's sake.

Then a more startling thought came to her. He might not recover. He had been well enough to speak, but the wound was serious. Madeleine knew the following two days would foretell what was to come. The earl could easily weaken and die.

Madeleine wished more than anything that he would not die. But she reminded herself that was only natural. She wished him to live for her family's sake.

Madeleine went to the bedstead and pulled the coverlet over his chest. She guessed it would be many hours before he woke again.

Despite herself, she brushed away the curl that rested on his forehead.

She could do no good here for the next hours. Madeleine slipped out of the room and down the stairs to the great hall.

The Baroness and Alfred sat by the fire. Juliana stood by the far window.

The Baroness rose as Madeleine entered. "How does he? Godfrey said he has awakened. Will he live? Did he speak?"

Madeleine laid her hand on her mother's arm. "Sit down. You are distraught."

Agnes hurried in with a pitcher of ale. Madeleine took it from her and set it on the table. "Go and sit with Lord Beaumont," Madeleine said to Agnes. "Come for me when he wakes."

The Baroness had sunk back into her chair. Juliana wandered over. Alfred had not moved. He sat and stared into the fire.

Madeleine said, "The earl sleeps now. If he does not develop a fever, he should live."

"Is not Sir Richard noble? Juliana said. "He has told us he shall ride all night. To think! He shall risk his life against murderers and cut-purses to save his friend."

"Fie on Sir Richard," the Baroness said.

Alfred stirred himself. "Really, Juliana. Did you not hear the man's threats against me? That if the earl should die, I should shortly follow him to the grave?"

Juliana waved her hand, as if killing Alfred were a mere trifle compared to facing murderers and cut-purses on the road.

"Alfred," the Baroness said, "it would be well for you to move to the Inn. At least until everything has...settled down."

"I must disagree, Aunt. I have my duty here. When the earl wakes again, I shall make my apologies for this, this...untoward accident."

Madeleine had heard enough. "Untoward accident? Cousin, I can say most decidedly, the earl would not wish to see you."

Alfred smiled in that condescending way Madeleine found maddening. "My dear, you do not understand honor among men. Trust to my superior judgment."

Madeleine wanted to scream that there had never been, and never could be, anything superior in Alfred's judgment. Instead she said, "I promise you, he would find it intolerable."

The Baroness said, "Alfred. I must insist. Go to the Inn. I shall send for you when it is right you return."

In a sulking tone, Alfred said, "Very well. I trust Madeleine shall visit me."

The Baroness looked about to speak. Madeleine stepped in front of her chair. "I shall be quite engaged. Tending to your victim. My mother and sister do not care for the sight of blood."

Juliana nodded. "Dear, no. We do not."

Alfred was finally convinced to go, and convinced he would have no visitors from the castle. He would have to find a means of entertaining himself. Alfred swore he could not do it, he had never done it. The Baroness would hear no more and walked him out the door.

The women spent the next hours in the bower. They were each meant to be working on embroidery pieces. Usually, it was only Madeleine who could not keep her mind on it. This day, both Madeleine and Juliana fidgeted, paced the room, picked up fabric and put it down again.

Even the Baroness could not put in many stitches. She lay her sewing aside. "I accomplish little," she said. "I shall take a turn in the garden." The Baroness rose and left Madeleine and Juliana alone.

Madeleine threw her sewing on the bed. "Juliana. You do not like Beaumont." She felt it unnecessary to point out that Beaumont did not like her either, though it pleased her to think of it.

Juliana flushed. "What can you mean?"

"I mean you do not like him enough to marry him."

Juliana shrugged. "He is an earl. He is rich."

"But there is one whom you do like."

Juliana turned from Madeleine and laughed. "I do not like anyone."

"You like Sir Richard."

Juliana whirled around. "Oh, so what if I do? Is it my fault Beaumont is so, so...him? Juliana said quietly, "Why could not Sir Richard be the rich earl?"

Madeleine said, "It is a pity he is not. But perhaps all shall come right in the end."

Juliana walked to the window and watched her mother stroll through the garden. "You think you know everything, Madeleine. You are so much more clever than I. You think it, do you not?"

Madeleine smiled. "Yes. I often do."

"But you are not always more clever. This shall not come right in the end. There is not a way for it to come right." Juliana sniffled and threw herself into a chair.

"I believe there is," Madeleine said.

Juliana waved her hand. Then she narrowed her eyes. "Do not you dare speak to mother about Sir Richard. I would pull out every last hair on your head."

Madeleine was about to answer, and not very nicely, when Agnes stumbled into the room.

Agnes flung herself into an undisciplined curtsy. "The beast has awakened."

Madeleine did her best to look annoyed. "Very well. I shall see to him. Have Godfrey prepare a beef broth and bring it to his room."

Agnes left muttering, "I know I ain't bringin' it. Wherever that man be, I'll be going the other direction."

Madeleine went back up the stairs to Beaumont's chamber. She slipped in soundlessly. The sun had passed to the other side of the castle and the light in the room had faded. She lit the sconces.

Beaumont lay with his eyes closed. Madeleine stole glances at him, but was careful not to stare. She was not certain if he slept again or merely rested.

Madeleine sat in a chair. She should have brought some embroidery with her. At least she could pretend to be doing something. As it was, she felt awkward just sitting there, not knowing where to look.

Madeleine noticed the counterpane that covered Beaumont had fallen down over his shoulders. Surely he slept, else he would be cold. She crept over and pulled the coverlet up to his neck.

Beaumont, with his eyes still closed, said, "Thank you."

Madeleine jumped. "I did not think you awake."

Beaumont opened his eyes. "I merely rested to recover from...what is her name? Agatha? She fluffed my pillow and chattered me nearly to my grave."

"I am afraid she is not nearly so fond of you, as you are of her," Madeleine said.

Beaumont raised his brows.

Madeleine felt herself flush. "No matter. Are you feeling better?"

Beaumont shifted on the pallet. "For having been skewered, I cannot say I feel as bad as I would have expected."

Madeleine looked away. She could not bear to speak of Alfred.

Beaumont sighed. "Very well. It was an accident."

Madeleine stared at the far wall and said nothing.

"I harbor no ill will toward your cousin."

Madeleine turned to face him. "Truly? You do not?"

"Well. Not for nearly killing me. His company is another matter." Beaumont smiled to himself. "I rather pity him. I imagine Richard went hard upon him."

"Sir Richard told my cousin that if you should die, Alfred would shortly follow," Madeleine said.

Beaumont laughed out loud. Then clutched his wound and winced. "Sir Richard is a true friend."

This was one thing Madeleine felt she and the earl could agree on. "He is, indeed," she said. "He rides all this night to fetch the surgeon. Sir Richard is a good man."

Beaumont's face flickered irritation. "Women always do like him. Your admiration cannot be surprising."

"I admire his friendship."

They sat silent. Madeleine was at a loss. What was she to say to this man? He was so impossible! How could he be irritated that she had commended the friend he himself had just spoken so highly of?

Then an idea came to her. He was jealous of her approbation of Sir Richard. Madeleine said, "Of course, it is of great benefit to Sir Richard to have such a friend as you. He has told me so himself."

Beaumont looked confused. "He has told you of the living? He knows I do not like it spoken of."

Madeleine was startled. "The living? No, indeed, he did not."

"Oh."

"What living?"

Beaumont sighed. "Well, now it appears I have told you myself. I convinced my father to take him on. To grant him the management of an estate."

"Why?" Madeleine asked.

"Because he was growing thin earning purses at tournaments."

"No," Madeleine stammered, "that is not what I meant. Why do not you wish it spoken of? Why cannot it be known?"

Beaumont did not answer immediately. Finally, he said, "I do not know. It just pleased me that we not speak of it."

"But you cannot think he befriends you for the gain of an estate?"

Beaumont smiled. "No, I do not think it. I suspect you would consider that a high price to pay for a mere estate."

They lapsed into silence.

Beaumont was a strange man, Madeleine thought. He was so unpleasant in manner. And then, when he did do something pleasant, it was not to be spoken of. She felt her cheeks grow hot as she thought of what Alfred would do in such a situation. Alfred would shout it to all who would listen. No one, particularly not the poor receiver of such a favor, would be permitted to forget it for an instant.

Madeleine shook her head as if to clear those thoughts away. What had been the point of thinking on it? Alfred would never confer such a favor to anyone.

Beaumont regarded her with an amused smile. Why did that smile always make her so angry? She said, "There are many knights who grow thin living on tournament purses. How came you to single out Sir Richard?"

"Sir Richard and I have known each other for some years. I understand his character. As he understands mine."

Madeleine wondered if she were beginning to understand Beaumont's character. Only a day ago, she would not have dreamed that he could be generous enough to help a friend in such a way. Or that he would forgive her idiotic cousin for nearly killing him. She did not know what to think.

The rest of the afternoon passed quietly. Godfrey brought a bowl of beef broth and Beaumont was able to sit up without too much pain. When he slept, Madeleine crept down to the kitchens.

Godfrey was directing the scullions as they loaded loaves of bread in the ovens. The scullions saw Madeleine and bowed, blushing. Godfrey said, "A'right ya two layabouts, go gather the eggs from the hen house."

The younger scullion, a boy of eleven years whose voice had not yet changed, pointed to a basket of eggs. "We done that this morn, Master Godfrey. We always do that in the morn."

Godfrey looked with consternation at the basket of eggs. "And ye think them hens are done laying for the day cause ya been there once this morn?"

The older scullion blinked, as if he'd just managed to catch on to Godfrey's meaning. "Come, you," he said, leading the puzzled boy away.

Godfrey sat down and his knees creaked. "Never were two denser kitchen boys. I'll never make anything outta them."

Madeleine sat next to him. She desperately wanted to tell Godfrey all that was on her mind, but could not think how to go about it.

Godfrey said, "I gather Lord Sneer recovers nicely."

Madeleine said, "Yes. It seems so." Her mind raced as she tried to look unconcerned. How was she to explain that things might have...changed? Godfrey had such a low opinion of the earl. And he had acquired that low opinion from Madeleine.

"And I 'spose he abused both me and me broth after I left. Did he accuse me 'a poison again?"

"No, indeed, he did not," Madeleine said.

Godfrey stretched his hands in front of him and cracked his knuckles. "Must a been tired. I expect he be makin' up for it when he's well enough."

"Godfrey..."

Godfrey folded his arms and waited for Madeleine to speak. She stared at the floor.

"A'right gal. What be ailing you? You look like yer 'bout to confess a murder."

"It is nearly that bad," Madeleine said softly.

"What? Speak up." Godfrey said.

Madeleine picked at a speck on her gown and said, "Lord Beaumont may not be quite as horrible as we first imagined."

"Hah! That's rich." Godfrey said.

"It is just...there are things we did not know," Madeleine said. "That we could not have known."

"We?" Godfrey asked. "I don' recollect forming a decided opinion on the matter. What I recollect is yer telling me what our opinion was based on yer own astute observations."

"Yes. Well. The point is, the earl has forgiven Alfred for the accident. And I discovered the earl has given Sir Richard a living."

"So he ain't the black-souled earl after all?" Godfrey said.

Madeleine felt herself flush. "No."

"And Sir Richard's got 'imself an income?"

"Enough to creditably support himself I think," Madeleine said.

"Enough to rescue the Baroness from financial ruin?" Godfrey asked.

"No," Madeleine said. "Not as much as that."

"Well, that's a pity, seeing as Juliana is partial to him. But if the earl ain't as bad as you thought, you can have no qualms 'bout Juliana marrying the man. Then you can send Alfred packin'. 'It be a blessin' all round."

"Yes." Madeleine desperately wanted to tell Godfrey that Beaumont had thought to marry her, not Juliana. But then she could not find the words. Madeleine comforted herself with the thought that it might be best to give Godfrey time to warm up to this new opinion of Beaumont.

Chapter Ten – The Summons

Madeleine planned to sit up during the night in case the earl developed a fever. She knew how it would be if it came on. He would seem to improve one moment, then the next his thoughts would muddle and his skin catch fire. She had seen fever take a man in a matter of hours.

Godfrey wouldn't hear of it. He ordered Madeleine up to the bower to get some rest. "You leave the man to me. If I need ya, I be wakin' ya."

She had not wanted to go. But once she was in bed with the heavy counterpane tucked under her chin, not even Juliana's kicking could keep her from sleep.

Loud banging jolted Madeleine awake. She sat up, trying to work out if she had been dreaming. The bower window had lightened to a pale pre-dawn grey. She heard nothing more and sank back down.

The banging started again. Certain she was awake now, Madeleine jumped from the bed and struggled into her gown.

Juliana rolled over and mumbled, "Who makes that racket?"

The Baroness did not stir.

Below, Godfrey shouted, "Who calls at the castle at this hour? If ye be thieves, we are many men and well-armed."

Cuthbert's voice came muffled through the heavily barred door. "Sir Richard and a gentleman have just ridden into the yard. I let 'em in meself."

"Sir Richard!" Juliana cried. She flew out of bed as if a mighty hand had yanked her out.

Madeleine was out the door as Juliana flung herself on her mother's bed. "Wake up! Get up, get up!"

By the time Madeleine had descended the staircase, Sir Richard was in the door. He had Godfrey by the surcoat. "Does he live?"

"He be sleepin' like a babe. Leastwise he was 'til you came chargin' at the door," Godfrey said.

Sir Richard let go of Godfrey and slumped. His face was ashen and he had a cut across his cheek. He muttered, "Forgive me, I rode all night not knowing..."

Madeleine hurried over to him. "Sir Richard, what happened to you?"

He looked at her dumbly.

"Your cheek. It is cut."

Sir Richard rubbed his cheek with the back of his hand. "A troublesome tree branch sought to delay my progress."

Madeleine heard a clearing of the throat behind Sir Richard.

Sir Richard started. "Right. I nearly forgot in my relief to get here." He stepped out of the doorway. "May I present the surgeon Ben Gundon."

Madeleine curtsied. "Good of you to come, sir."

Gundon pulled twigs and leaves from his hair as he bowed. "Delighted. It has been a most interesting evening. I suggested to this gentleman that we might begin our journey at daybreak. As you see, that was not to be."

88

Madeline bit her lip. He was a funny little man. He was shorter than even Juliana and had wild black curls sprouting from his head in all directions. The remaining twigs and leaves did not enhance his appearance.

Juliana flew down the stairs with the sleepy Baroness trailing behind her. "Sir Richard!" Juliana cried. Then she blushed and looked at the floor.

Sir Richard bowed.

"Your face," Juliana said, staring at the cut.

The Baroness narrowed her eyes at Juliana. "It is but a scratch."

"Indeed. It is of no consequence," Sir Richard said. "May I present Ben Gundon."

The Baroness and Juliana curtsied. "I trust you shall find our patient has been well tended," the Baroness said to the surgeon.

Gundon bowed. "I have no fear of that, M'lady."

"Your face," Juliana said to Sir Richard. "It must hurt terribly."

Sir Richard blushed.

Madeleine saw she would need to move things along. She turned to the surgeon, "You have had a tiring journey, but perhaps you would look in on the earl before you rest?"

"Certainly." The surgeon said. "I trust the earl shan't mind that I carry half of Danglen's forests in my hair."

"Godfrey, please show him up." Madeleine said. "Then bring him ale, bread and cheese from the kitchen."

Godfrey led Gundon up the stairs. Madeleine turned to Sir Richard. "Come to the kitchens with me. I shall see to your cut."

"I could see to it," Juliana said.

The Baroness tightened her lips. "Nonsense, Juliana. Madeleine shall do it. You may retire to the bower with me."

89

Juliana looked about to protest. Sir Richard said, "It is not a fit sight for such a delicate sensibility."

Madeleine rolled her eyes and led Sir Richard away before either he or Juliana could appear any more foolish than they already did.

In the kitchen, Madeleine sat Sir Richard down on a stool. She stoked the fire to heat some water. "You must be exhausted."

Sir Richard sat with his head hanging down. "Exhausted? No, I am perfectly fine." He looked up. "How does he? The truth, Madeleine. How does he really?"

Madeleine handed his a cup of ale. "He has no fever. And his tongue is as sharp as ever."

"Is it? A good sign, I am sure."

Madeleine laughed. "Not many would count that a good sign."

"Ah. But you have spent time with him now," Sir Richard said. "Do not you begin to see the worthy character beneath the thorns?"

Madeleine blushed and turned away. "Perhaps."

Sir Richard took a big swig of ale and put his cup down. "I was certain you would. He claimed you liked him not. I counseled him to but give it time."

"I did not say I liked him." Madeleine said.

"But you did not say you did not," Sir Richard said with a smile. "That is encouragement enough."

"I do not mean to encourage him," Madeleine said.

What was she saying? She certainly did mean to encourage him.

"You are too modest for that. Yet, I understand you perfectly," Sir Richard said.

Madeleine grabbed a piece of linen and dipped it into the water heating on the fire. "Enough of that. Let me see your face." She dabbed at the cut, washing off the dirt from the overnight ride. "It is not deep. It should heal well."

Sir Richard smiled at her. "Your face is very red."

"It is always hot in the kitchens," Madeleine said.

"I am eager to see my friend," Sir Richard said. "I have much to tell him."

Madeleine wanted to disappear into the ground. She guessed Sir Richard would tell Beaumont he might be encouraged. It was exactly what she had wanted. But now that it was about to happen, her stomach felt as if a thousand wings beat to get out. She did not like it.

"You'll not see him now," Madeleine said. "You shall go and rest this instant. I will hear what Gundon has to say when he is finished."

Sir Richard smirked as he stood up. He made an elaborate bow. "As you say, Lady Beaumont. He laughed and left her alone.

Madeleine was mortified. It had all seemed perfectly reasonable. Marry Beaumont and everyone would benefit. But could she really? What would it be like? Could she make some sort of life with him? And if it were not bad enough that Sir Richard laughed at her. What would Godfrey say? For that matter, what would her mother say?

Madeleine sat and stared into the fire. She had proclaimed far and wide, including to the man himself, that she did not like him. But, in truth, she did. How could it be so? He was not at all like the man she imagined she would marry. That man was a gentleman, courteous to all. And dark-haired. Yet, she did like Beaumont.

Godfrey interrupted her musings. "Gundon has done. He is just consulting with Sir Richard. Far as I can figure, the great man should be right enough after a few days' rest."

Madeleine started. "Sir Richard? I bid him go directly to bed."

"Then what ya told him, and what he done, be two different matters."

Madeleine stamped her foot. "Why cannot he do as he is asked?"

Godfrey laughed. "He be a grown man. I expect if he don't wanna be abed, not a female in the world that can make 'im."

Gundon walked into the kitchen. He bowed. "I am pleased to tell you I find your illustrious house guest on the mend. We must merely get him through the next several days. Should no fever develop, we may consider ourselves in the clear."

Madeleine said, "Thank you, sir."

Gundon waved a short arm. "Nonsense. Pleasure. Naturally, we must keep him quiet. Any sort of agitation could easily bring a turn for the worse."

Madeleine nodded. "Yes, of course."

"I am at your service until the danger has passed," the surgeon said. "I would be up with the earl still, but his friend pushed me out of the room most unceremoniously."

Madeleine felt her heart drop.

"No matter. I can bleed him later."

Madeleine cringed. The deClare's own physician liked to do the same. Whether a stomach ailment or broken bone, blood must be let out. Humours must be balanced. Madeleine had never seen the benefit of it. It always seemed to make the patient worse.

"Must you bleed him?" she asked.

"I detect an overabundance of choleric humour," Gundon said. "It must be released."

Madeleine did not think it worth mentioning that Beaumont's humours always tended toward the choleric.

Sir Richard bounded into the kitchen. Before he could speak, Gundon said, "Has he taken a turn?"

Sir Richard laughed. "A turn for the better, I should think."

"I shall go immediately and make my own assessment," the surgeon said.

Sir Richard laid his hand on the surgeon's arm. "No, my good man. He asks for Madeleine."

Madeleine felt as if she would faint. Would no one give her a minute to collect herself? Why were things rushing along so fast?

"A noble sentiment," Gundon said. "The earl cannot but appreciate what the lady has done for him. But I must bleed him. It really cannot wait."

Madeleine said, "Yes, Sir Richard. It really cannot be put off." Had she just said that?

"Nonsense," Sir Richard said. He turned to Gundon. "The earl is most decided. He wishes to see Madeleine. You may bleed him later."

Chapter Eleven – A Sudden Departure

Madeleine trudged up the stairs. Every other day, she felt there were far too many stairs. This day, she felt there were far too few. Terror gripped her insides. What would Beaumont say? What would she say? She had determined she would say yes. But could she manage it without sounding like an idiot?

And when it was done! Her mother would be sent for and asked for her approval. What would she say? Then all in the castle would know. Godfrey would think she had gone mad. Alfred would be told. And her uncle.

Madeleine stopped half way up the staircase. Indeed, she should not go. It was too much trouble for everyone. She turned around. She had decided she would ask Cuthbert to hide her somewhere.

Sir Richard stood with his arms crossed at the bottom of the stairs. With a small smile, he said, "You make excellent progress. I do not know when I have ever seen you ascend the stairs so well."

Madeleine glared at him. The beast. How had she ever thought him so wonderful? If she ran and hid now, he would tell all in the castle. Madeleine could see it in his face.

Madeleine flipped her hair over her shoulder, turned and marched up the stairs.

Madeleine decided she was being ridiculous. Why should she tremble? She need not make a speech and wait for an answer. She need only answer. And if she could not speak, a nod would have to do.

Madeleine pushed open the door. No, she was not afraid.

Beaumont sat up, pillows piled behind him. His blond curls were tousled, which suddenly struck Madeleine as remarkably wonderful.

"I thank you for attending me so quickly," the earl said.

Madeleine stared at the floor.

"Please," the earl said. "Sit down."

Madeleine walked to the chair, sat down and folded her hands.

Beaumont cleared his throat. "I asked you to attend me...I feel I must tell you of certain...thoughts I have had.

Madeleine examined her hands, as if she were mesmerized by them. She willed him to hurry on.

Beaumont continued. "As you are aware, your relations are not quite what I would wish to connect myself with. Your household lacks the proper dignity that I require."

Madeleine bristled. What had he just said?

"It is a credit to you that you note these things so distinctly. You are as a rose among weeds."

The deClares were weeds? How dare he?

"Naturally, you have been too delicate to speak of it forthrightly. That is proper. Indeed, I would expect nothing less. But it is all too evident," the earl continued.

The arrogance!

"So I would wish to offer you a future that would more closely suit your natural taste and refinement of mind."

The earl was still speaking, but Madeleine could not hear him anymore. A thousand oceans crashed in her ears. Where were the complements? What kind of proposal was this?

Madeleine jumped from her chair. "If you believe for one moment that I disdain my own relatives, you are quite mistaken. You are unfeeling and ungentlemanly. I have sought, since you first crossed our threshold, to prevent Juliana from attaching herself to you. So she would not be miserable forever."

The earl stared at her; he looked as if he had been struck.

She threw her chin up. "M'lord. You may take your lack of manners back to your dignified household."

Madeleine burst into tears and ran from the room. She stumbled down the corridor and paused before she reached the bower door. Madeleine wiped her face. Her mother and Juliana could never know of this. She could not bear to ever have it spoken of. She trusted Sir Richard would not reveal any of it, once he had spoken with Beaumont.

She took a deep breath and entered the bower.

Juliana sat on the window seat as Agnes brushed her hair. The Baroness reclined on her bed, already dressed for the day.

"Good heavens, Madeleine," the Baroness said. "What is the matter? Is it the earl?"

"No," Madeleine said. "I've a headache. It is no matter."

"Agnes," the Baroness said, "ask Godfrey to boil a willow bark tea."

"No," Madeleine said, in a sharp tone. "I am perfectly fine. I must just rest."

Madeleine crawled under the counterpane and squeezed her eyes shut. If her mother and sister would only go away!

Shouting echoed from the first floor of the castle. Madeleine opened her eyes. The Baroness rose from her bed and shook out her gown. "By the saints!" she said. "What can be happening now? There has never been so much disturbance in a single day."

The Baroness and Juliana hurried to the doorway.

Madeleine heard the surgeon say, "But you cannot, M'lord! The journey will kill you!"

Beaumont's voice answered back. "Out of my way, sir. Richard, bring the horses."

The Baroness called down the staircase. "Lord Beaumont, what has happened?"

"My apologies, Baroness," the earl said. "I find I must leave this instant."

"This instant? Has a message come?" the Baroness asked.

Madeleine heard her mother and Juliana hurry down the stairs. She put her head under the pillow so she would not hear more.

Madeleine lay there for what seemed hours. So Beaumont had taken her at her word. He would leave immediately. She had ruined everything. No. He had ruined everything. Poor Juliana! She would be heartbroken to say goodbye to Sir Richard.

Madeleine felt guilt crawl around her insides. Oh, if she had not lost her temper! But no, how could she not? How could she listen to such a speech and say nothing?

Why should she feel sad? Beaumont was horrible. Madeleine had known that from the first. To offer for her hand in such a way! As if she were to be pitied. It pained her to realize that she had often thought that herself. But how dare he?

And to slink off like a beaten cur. Sir Richard would not have run away from one rejection, she was certain. He would have stayed and tried again. But not Beaumont. Not with his kind of pride. Why had he ever come here?

Madeleine's heart sank further as she thought of the future. There would be no escape from Alfred now. The household's survival would depend on it. Why had not she thought of that before telling Beaumont to go away?

The Baroness bustled into the room. "Madeleine. Do you still lie there? The household is in an uproar."

Madeleine sat up. "So he is gone, then?"

The Baroness sighed. "Yes. He is gone. And what has possessed the man, I cannot fathom."

Madeleine was silent.

"Juliana is distraught. She paces the great hall and refuses to come and rest."

Madeleine felt her eyes prick. She felt worse than ever about what she had done to Juliana. "Perhaps she shall recover quickly, mother. After all, there must be many earls who would seek her hand."

Her mother looked at her with consternation. "Juliana's hopes are ruined. There are not many earls in the whole of Danglen. And there are certainly not many earls of marriageable age who are not already married!"

Madeleine rose and took her mother's hand. "In truth, mother, I do not think she would have been happy with him."

Her mother shook her off. "Cease your romantic ramblings. It would have been a brilliant match. And we desperately needed it, as you well know."

Madeleine turned away.

The Baroness said, "At least we have Alfred. We are not completely undone." The Baroness paced the room. "But what got into that inscrutable man? I never saw the like of it."

Madeleine said softly, "He said nothing, then?"

"Nothing illuminating, I assure you. He wove around the hall like a drunken man, he could barely stand. Sir Richard nearly carried him to the stables. Other than, 'my apologies, I must go' he had nothing to say at all."

"How very strange," Madeleine mumbled.

"I do not see how he expects to sit a horse in that condition," the Baroness said. "And Sir Richard would say nothing."

Madeleine breathed a sigh of relief. Sir Richard had not revealed what he knew. Madeleine might be miserable, but she would be the only one to know it.

"It is all a result of the accident, I suppose," the Baroness said. "The earl began to regain his strength and he regained his temper with it. How foolish! It cannot be Juliana's fault that her cousin is not a practiced bowman."

The Baroness stamped her foot. "I must have an answer to this. I shall write the earl and demand an explanation."

Madeleine's breath caught. "Surely, that is not wise." She appealed to her mother's pride. "He has insulted us. To beg a reason would be an embarrassment."

The Baroness seemed to consider this. "Quite right. It is best the earl believe we feel well rid of him."

Madeleine stroked her mother's hair. "And we do, dear. Earl or not, he was rude and horrible. Juliana deserves better. And she shall have better. I am certain of it."

The Baroness seemed to relax. "No doubt, you are right. If only we can convince Juliana."

Madeleine wondered how her mother had not seen it was Sir Richard that had captured Juliana's heart.

The Baroness patted her curls into place. "Well. What is done is done. It is the future we must consider. Tell the stable boy to ride to the Inn. Alfred may return."

Madeleine thought quickly. She could not imagine having to bear Alfred this day. "Juliana is too distraught, mother. Surely, we must give her at least a day to recover before we subject her, I mean before she must entertain...anyone."

The Baroness narrowed her eyes. "You shall not avoid Alfred indefinitely, Madeleine. You understand your duty."

Madeleine nodded. It broke her heart and made her cringe at the same time. But she did, indeed, understand her duty.

The Baroness smiled. "Very well. The morrow shall be soon enough."

Chapter Twelve – The Anonymous Package

The Baroness left the bower to speak with the servants and swear them to silence on the matter of the earl's abrupt departure. Madeleine knew it was hopeless, though she did not say so. She was certain Agnes would spread the tale far and wide. Madeleine wondered how they would manage to show their faces in the village. She guessed there would be endless whispering, smirking and giggling at the deClare's expense.

Madeleine felt as if all the blood had drained from her body. She had no strength to get up. Her future was laid before her and it was as bleak as any could be. A lifetime with Alfred to pay for a moment of temper.

Would she could turn back time! If she could have held her tongue! Then she would face a life with Beaumont. It would have been difficult; he was a difficult man. But at least he was educated and pleasing to look at. She began to think that her threat of entering a nunnery was an attractive alternative. It would be a more pleasant future, she was sure.

And why should she be responsible for saving her family from financial ruin? If her mother had just paid more attention to the running of the estate they would not teeter on the brink of disaster. Perhaps she should leave her mother and Juliana to fend for themselves. Juliana could marry Alfred. Or not. They could do what they liked.

But, no. Madeleine could not do that. The truth, the truth they did not know, was that she had ruined them all, from her own silly pride. She had spent so many years feeling superior that just when she should have swallowed her pride to gain a good end, she could not control herself. And worse, Madeleine had always criticized Juliana so harshly for being self-indulgent. In the end, it had been Madeleine's own self-indulgence that would provide all the miserable years to come.

Juliana burst into the bower. Her face was ashen and her hair disheveled. She pointed a finger at Madeleine. "How could you do it?"

Madeleine sat up. "What?"

Juliana threw herself on her mother's bed. "Do not gaze at me as if you do not have the first idea of what I mean."

"But, truly, I do not." Madeleine had a sinking feeling in her stomach. It was not possible Juliana knew what had transpired with Beaumont..

Juliana glared at her. "Sir Richard told me that Beaumont would propose to you."

Madeleine felt her face grow hot. She did not know how to answer.

"And you refused him, did you not? That is why they left?"

"Yes," Madeleine whispered.

Juliana launched herself at Madeleine. She pulled at her hair. "You selfish brat!" She straddled Madeleine and pinned her shoulders to the bed. Madeleine was far stronger, but felt she had nothing left to fight with.

Juliana squeezed Madeleine's shoulders until they ached. "I should have known. Madeleine is too good for anybody. Madeleine is smarter and more clever than anybody. Madeleine is so proud, not even an earl can impress."

Juliana was crying now. Madeleine said, "Do not say more, Juliana. I cannot bear it."

"You cannot bear it? You?" She slapped Madeleine across the face. "You have ruined my life and you cannot bear it?"

Madeleine's cheek stung, but she felt powerless to do anything.

Juliana jumped off her and stamped around the bower. "You just wait, madam clever. Wait until mother hears just how clever you have been."

"You would not tell her," Madeleine said. "There can be no point to it."

"I certainly shall tell her. She deserves to know what sort of viper she owns as a daughter," Juliana said.

Madeleine felt her temper rise. "Juliana. If you tell her, the whole story must come out. Do you really wish her to know that you love Sir Richard?"

Juliana sank down on the window seat and began to sob.

Madeleine got up and sat next to her. She hugged Juliana's shoulders. "Since you know this much, you may as well know all. It may make you feel better to know how miserable I have made myself, as well as you."

Juliana turned to her, wiping the tears from her cheeks.

"I meant to say yes. I still cannot fathom how I did not. So now I must marry Alfred. I know you are heartbroken to lose Sir Richard. But surely, that is worse."

Juliana sniffled. "Oh, Madeleine. Why did you do it? When all might have turned out so well?"

Madeleine sighed. She had just managed to figure that out. "Because I am not so clever as I used to think."

They sat in silence for a few minutes. Finally, Madeleine said, "You should not despair, Juliana. I do not think Sir Richard shall disappear forever. He is not the sort. And after I have married...Alfred, and our money troubles are behind us, we can broach the idea to mother."

Juliana looked at her with a hopeful expression. "Do you really think it?"

"Yes. I do. Mother will at first be shocked, but she does indeed like the man. And she can have no arguments against it when we have silver in the chest."

"Of course, I have been silly, have I not? Richard shall find a way around this difficulty. He is so clever." She reddened. "Not clever like you. But a different sort."

Madeleine nodded. "Yes. His is of the right sort."

Juliana patted Madeleine's hand. "You are well rid of Beaumont. I never met such a proud and disagreeable man. It is a pity Sir Richard is so attached to him. You do think Sir Richard shall be back?"

Madeleine saw Juliana was regaining her usual spirits. She said, "Indeed. I do."

The next days passed in near silence. Alfred returned, but the ladies of the castle drifted, ghost-like, from room to room. Much as he tried, Alfred could not engage anyone in conversation.

Madeleine spent most of her time in the kitchens, knowing Alfred would never venture there. Although she knew she must accept him, she delayed the inevitable. Madeleine dodged Godfrey's questions about the earl. Godfrey finally concluded it was good riddance. Madeleine pretended to agree and hoped that would be the end of it. Godfrey did not know she had determined to marry Alfred. Madeleine could not bear to hear all the reasons against it. She already knew them.

Juliana spent her days at one window, then another. She eagerly watched when a rider trotted into the yard, then sighed when it was only a peddler or smithy.

The Baroness worked on her embroidery and eyed Juliana. She eyed Madeleine when she could find her. The Baroness answered all of Alfred's questions with 'Yes, certainly'.

Toward dusk on the third day, Madeleine sat with her mother. The Baroness had sent Agnes to drag her from the kitchen. Alfred had been prevailed upon to run an errand to the village; he had gone with much grumbling.

The Baroness said, "Madeleine. You cannot hide forever. You must give Alfred an opportunity."

Madeleine bent her head over her sewing and jabbed the needle into the fabric.

The Baroness sighed. "Alfred does not fit your romantic notions. Perhaps you have been too protected thus far. You would not find him such an unpleasant duty if you knew what it was to starve."

Madeleine ripped out the stitches she had just put in.

The Baroness threw down her embroidery. Through gritted teeth, she said, "It is time you grew up."

Madeleine was about to answer, she had not determined exactly what except it should be sharp, when Juliana cried, "A rider!"

The Baroness sighed. "Yes, my dear. We have many riders to the castle. As I mentioned just a moment ago. It is not the earl. Please get that from your head."

"How strange," Juliana said. "He wears livery, but I do not recognize it."

The Baroness and Madeleine ran to the window. If there were livery, it was no peddler.

Madeleine saw a tall, blond young man jump off a fit chestnut destrier. She did not recognize the man or the green and yellow livery.

"Come, girls. Take up your sewing," the Baroness said. "We must not look like bumpkins staring out the window."

They sat and pretended to sew, waiting for the mysterious man to be announced.

Agnes stumbled in with the man following her. She said to the Baroness, "This gentleman asks to see you." She glanced behind her. "He don't give no name. Just so ya don't think I forgot to ask it."

The Baroness rose. "Agnes, you may go."

Agnes turned and gave the stranger one last suspicious look.

The man stood before them. He seemed in his twenties and carried himself as a gentleman. He carried a large leather satchel and bowed awkwardly under its weight.

He said, "M'lady, I was entrusted to bring you this package."

The women curtsied. Juliana burst out, "Is there a letter?"

The Baroness gave Juliana a sharp look.

"I do not know," the man answered.

"What is your name, sir, and from whom do you come?" the Baroness asked.

"My apologies. I am not at liberty to give my name and, in truth, I do not know what I carry." He addressed the Baroness, but glanced at Madeleine.

"This is most unusual, sir. What are we to make of it? A gentleman would certainly give his name." the Baroness said.

The man smiled. "You are right. And yet I was sworn not to reveal my name, so I cannot."

The Baroness' face showed irritation. "What are we to do with you then? How are we to entertain you or offer you supper if we do not know who you are? We are women alone, we cannot risk such an impropriety."

"I appreciate your delicacy, Baroness." The man said. "But I cannot stay. I was charged to deliver this and be gone immediately." He bowed. "Good day, M'ladies."

He laid the satchel on a side table, turned on his heel and was gone.

Juliana raced to the window to watch him go. The Baroness stared at where the man had been.

Madeleine's heart was in her throat. The man had resembled Beaumont. The Baroness and Juliana did not seem as if they had noted it. She shook herself. She was absurd. Her grief had given flight to her imagination. She said, "Well. Perhaps we should see what that mysterious man has delivered."

The Baroness walked over to the satchel and opened it. She gasped.

"What is it?" Madeleine asked.

The Baroness turned. Her face was white. "It is silver. The satchel is filled with silver."

Chapter Thirteen – The Road to Bellham

Madeleine stared at her mother. Neither of them spoke.

Agnes burst into the room. She curtsied. "Here's another of 'em. This one says he's from your brother."

A disheveled man bowed low. He said, "Message for your ladyship from Sir William Clancy." He held out a rolled parchment.

The Baroness took it and the messenger bowed himself from the room.

She quickly opened the parchment and scanned the contents. She sat down.

Juliana ran to her. "What is it? What does my uncle say?"

"We are all invited to Bellham," the Baroness said. "My brother has been delayed longer than he anticipated. He requires Alfred's help on a business matter. He would wish us to join him there. He has rented a house." She paused and looked up at Madeleine. "He says we may find Madeleine's trousseau in the more elegant shops of the city."

Madeleine cringed. She supposed her uncle had never had any doubt of her marrying Alfred.

"Bellham!" Juliana cried.

The Baroness said, "That explains the mysterious arrival of silver. My brother is too delicate to mention we could hardly afford such a journey, nor buy Madeleine what she requires."

Alfred entered the room, huffing and puffing. "I've done all you asked, Aunt. Though it was not easy. A bit here and a bob there, you would think somebody in that wretched village would have everything all together."

The women stared at him without answering.

He blinked. "What?"

The Baroness approached him and took his hands. "We have had wonderful news. Your father writes that we are all to come to Bellham."

Alfred shrugged. "All right."

The Baroness pointed at the satchel. "And he has been most kind. Most delicate. He has sent this silver by anonymous post."

"What," Alfred stuttered. He disengaged himself from the Baroness and looked inside the satchel. "God's blood, that is a good amount of silver. He gave it to you?"

"Please do not mention that we know it."

Alfred scratched his head. "Most unlike my father. Giving away money. I would never have thought it."

"We are all family, are we not?" The Baroness said. "And soon to be closer bound than ever."

An idea seemed to dawn on Alfred. He looked over at Madeleine with a silly grin. "Oh..."

"Well," the Baroness said, "we must begin the arrangements. We must pack and arrange a coach. Oh dear, so much to do. Madeleine, take the silver to the bower, separate the coins by type and put them into smaller carrying bags." The Baroness hugged herself. "There must be enough there to satisfy our creditors and pay for the journey. Juliana, see to the gowns and such. I shall inform Godfrey - he will travel with us for protection."

Alfred cleared his throat. "Aunt, you can look no further for a protector. I am at your service."

The Baroness seemed hardly to hear him. She waved him off. "Yes, certainly."

Madeleine carried the heavy satchel up the stairs and into the bower. Juliana busied herself emptying the contents of the garderobe and frowning at the lamentable state of their clothes.

Madeleine dumped the contents of the satchel onto the bed. Coins of every size and country spilled over the midnight blue counterpane. Shillings, francs, deniers, ducats, marks, florins and pennies glittered like so many stars in the sky. A small square of parchment fluttered to rest on the constellation of silver.

"What is that?" Juliana asked.

"I do not know," Madeleine said, unfolding the note.

She had to squint to read the tiny writing. It read: 'A rose without thorns is no rose at all.'

"Well? What does it say?"

Madeleine crumpled up the parchment. Her hands shook and she slid it under a pillow. She said, "Nothing. Just some scribble that has lain at the bottom of the satchel for years."

Juliana's hand darted under the pillow and snatched the parchment. "A rose without thorns is no rose at all?" She threw the parchment back at Madeleine. "Clearly not someone who understands flowers. If there were roses without thorns I am sure we would have put them in the garden."

Juliana went back to her sorting and frowning. Madeleine began to separate the coins, but had to start over several times. Could the silver be from Beaumont? Could the note be from him? It was true, the note might not have anything to do with the silver. But then again, it might.

When had her uncle ever sent money? He knew the straits they were in, and yet he had never relieved them before. Madeleine had always suspected he purposely did not, so as to ensure her marriage to Alfred.

But would it be like Beaumont to do it? She thought not. Perhaps it was Sir Richard's doing. He could not have much silver to spare, but might not he have convinced the earl to send it for Juliana's sake? That seemed more likely.

'A rose with no thorns is no rose at all'? What did it mean? Did it refer to her? Or Beaumont? Did Sir Richard write it as some sort of message?

Juliana said, "Bellham! Dinners and balls and balls and dinners! And Madeleine, Sir Richard said they were to go there directly from here. They were to pick up fabric and lace and such for the earl's mother and sister. He said the list was endless. Certainly it would take many days to complete. Do not you think?"

"I do not know. But Juliana, do not pin your hopes on seeing him. The earl shall travel in far different circles than our uncle."

"Oh fie, Madeleine. We are a respected family. I am certain we shall be invited to all the best houses."

Madeleine did not know if that were true or not. A poor Baroness and her two dowry-less daughters may be respectable, but perhaps not very interesting. And yet Juliana's beauty was renowned. Her mother had always said there was nothing society liked more than a new and pretty face.

Juliana said, "If we can only hurry there, we are sure to see him."

Madeleine sighed. The only thing this trip would bring her was an engagement to Alfred. It was one thing to dodge her cousin and her mother. It would be more difficult to do so with her hardheaded uncle.

The next three days were a flurry of activity. Godfrey arranged a coach. The Baroness sent letters with him to post. She intended on seeing every acquaintance she had ever known who would be in

Bellham. She sent an especially long letter to her old friend Countess deBarge. That, she said, would guarantee them an introduction to the best society.

The seamstress was sent for and she and six apprentices worked night and day. The Baroness said it was all well and good to have things made when they were in Bellham, but they must not arrive looking like shabby country bumpkins.

Madeleine tried to find enthusiasm for the trip. She wondered at herself. Up until now, the idea of Bellham and 'the best society' had sent shivers down her back. During the long and boring hours spent sewing in the bower, she had often rehearsed what she would say. What clever witticism she might utter to the fascination of all around her. She had thought her introduction to the world would somehow bring a new life.

Even her new ball gown could not excite. She knew it should. While the current rage was jewel tones and pastels, her gown was a deep, luxurious brown velvet. It was original and striking. The seamstress had even sewn in a hem, in case Madeleine managed to grow before she reached Bellham.

And still, she was without energy. The trip loomed as an unpleasant chore. A physician would have diagnosed Madeleine with melancholy and bled her directly.

As much as Madeleine would have preferred to stay in de Clare castle and sleep the days away, the morning of their departure arrived. The coachman, a fat and merry man that Godfrey had known from his childhood days, tied their trunks to the roof.

He hustled them into the coach. "Now there, it be tight. You two little ones on one side." He bowed to Madeleine. "You, M'lady, can have the other side to yourself."

By the saints, Madeleine thought. She was not a giant.

The coachman threw fur rugs on them and slammed the door. Godfrey jumped up in front with the driver. Alfred sat on his destrier

115

peering in the window. "Fear nothing, good ladies, I shall protect you from any dangers on the road."

Juliana giggled. The Baroness said, "Yes, yes, of course you shall."

Madeleine sunk back in her seat.

The coachman slapped the reins and they rolled out of the yard and down the long, oak lined avenue. They clip-clopped down the lane and through the village. A few of the villagers stood to wave them off. Most of them with smirks on their faces. Godfrey had told Madeleine that a rumour went round that they were off to chase the earl. She sank deeper in her seat.

They had not left the village before the Baroness was softly snoring. Madeleine wished she could as well.

"What shall you do when you see Beaumont?" Juliana asked.

"What?"

"What shall you do? What shall you say?"

"Nothing," Madeleine stuttered. "I mean to say, I will not see him."

"Of course you shall see him. I know Richard will find me. I do not know how, but I am sure he shall. He is a knight and he loves me. I am sure he shall contrive it. And where Richard goes, so does Beaumont." Juliana sat back with a satisfied smile.

"That is, it is just...ridiculous."

"Say what you like, but I know it. So what shall you say?"

"I have nothing to say to him." Madeleine said.

Juliana stared out the window for a moment. Then she took a deep breath. She said, "Why are you always so smug? As if you know everything and nobody else knows anything?"

Madeleine sat up straight and had her mouth open to answer. Juliana held up her hand. "No. Do not say anything. This time, I shall say what I want without you interrupting. You always twist my words so I seem foolish and then confuse me so I hardly know what I meant to say."

Madeleine sat back, for once speechless.

"You are the clever one," Juliana continued. "We all know it. Not a day goes by when it is not pointed out to me in some manner."

"What?" Madeleine said.

"Oh, do not look as if you do not comprehend what I say," Juliana said. "What do I hear from morning 'til evening? Do not worry yourself, Juliana, Madeleine will devise something. Madeleine, count the silver. Juliana, see to the gowns. But I am not as stupid as everyone thinks me. Richard does not think me stupid."

"But I never--" Madeleine stuttered.

"Oh, you never said it outright? Had I not comprehended the heavy hints all these years, I would be stupid indeed."

Madeleine did not know what to say. It was true, she had felt superior to Juliana. But she had thought it her little secret. Her compensation for Juliana being the pretty one. Madeleine said, "I suppose it is like how I feel because everyone calls you the pretty one."

Juliana flushed. "Pretty does not last. And anyway, you are pretty enough yourself. When you do not have knives on your tongue."

"What!"

The loudness of Madeleine's voice startled both of them. They looked over at the Baroness. She snuffled and turned her head, then sank back into gentle snoring.

"The point is, Madeleine, you think you are too good for anybody. You are prickly to a fault. You deserve nothing better than Alfred."

"Juliana, how can you say..."

"Because someone must."

The Baroness roused herself. "Must what?"

117

The rest of the morning passed quietly. Madeleine stared out the window at the world passing by. They rumbled down shady lanes, the oaks reaching over their heads in a roof of greenery. They rolled past well-tended asserts, the men busy pulling up roots to prepare for the spring planting season. They pulled in to noisy inn yards and exchanged horses. Madeleine saw it all, but she did not take it in.

The world did not make sense anymore. All she had known to be true now felt false. Juliana had given her counsel and pointed out her faults! Smug? That was ridiculous. Madeleine knew she was spirited. What intelligent young lady was not? But better than everyone else? Certainly not. Not everyone in the whole world anyway. And if Juliana knew why she had rejected Beaumont, that he had insulted her own family, she would not be so quick to condemn.

How dare Juliana! That empty-headed girl. She had never done anything for anybody. She had certainly never given Madeleine a thought.

Madeleine made every attempt to work herself to righteous anger. But a small idea kept niggling at her. Was she not as she saw herself? Was she not the put upon, but mentally superior younger sister? She was more clever than Juliana, she knew it. But had she advertised it as pointedly as Juliana suggested? And if she had... She could not think of that.

She tried to clear her mind. It had been a silly conversation, as conversations with Juliana usually were. But as firmly as she determined to dismiss it, there was a weight on her shoulders that had not been there before.

Chapter Fourteen – Clara Candlewick

The house Madeleine's uncle had rented sat just outside the city proper. Madeleine thought that was just as well. The stench from the town reached them even there. A mixture that smelled of urine, garbage and wet animal fur hung in the air. She could not imagine what it would be like to live any closer.

The dwelling was large, with a stone first floor and a wooden second. It was approached by a short but pleasing lane, shaded by mature oaks. The coachman reined in the horses as a stout man in a tight fitting surcoat came down the stone steps of the entry.

The Baroness poked her head out the window. "William!"

"Hello, my dear. Let us get you out. Your legs must be frozen in that cramped coach."

He swung the door open and helped down the Baroness. He gave his arm to Juliana. "Beautiful as ever, my dear." He grasped Madeleine's hand. "Look at you. So much grown!"

Madeleine stifled a sigh.

They were herded into the house, with a great deal of instructions given to Godfrey on what to do with the trunks. Finally, they were seated in a receiving room. Madeleine's uncle said, "Where is Alfred? Did he not accompany you?"

Madeleine looked around startled. She had forgotten all about him.

The Baroness looked equally mystified. "He did. Where can he be? How very strange."

A clatter of hooves drifted in from the drive. A few moments later, Alfred burst into the room. He was disheveled and out of breath.

"There you are, son. What detained you?"

Alfred caught his breath. He glanced at the Baroness. "Their servant, that Godfrey person, left me with the bill at the last inn. It took some time to convince the innkeeper that I would send the money to him. I do not know how that scoundrel and his coachman friend managed to drink so much ale in such a short time."

The Baroness' lips pressed together. Madeleine groaned.

"Well, no matter," Madeleine's uncle said. "You are here now."

Alfred threw himself into a chair. "Barely."

There was silence in the room. Madeleine's uncle stood up. "Sister," he said to the Baroness, "let me show you the house. Juliana, you may come as well."

Before she knew it, Madeleine was alone with Alfred. She stared out the window, hoping they could just remain silent. She supposed her uncle would use every opportunity to throw them together.

Alfred cleared his throat. He paced the room with his arms clasped behind his back.

Madeleine was surprised. For once Alfred had nothing to say.

He turned on his heel and faced Madeleine. "I realize you have anticipated my formal declaration. It cannot but be a frightening and exciting moment for a modest maid. But tremble no more. I--"

"No!"

"What?"

"I mean, there is no hurry. We have just arrived. And, and I feel a headache coming on."

"You have a lot of headaches," Alfred said, petulance in his voice.

"It is just that, that, I must have time. Time to...accept the idea."

Alfred returned to pacing the room. He stopped and scowled, as if something had just occurred to him. He blurted out, "I do not like you either!"

"What!"

He pointed a shaking finger at her. "There are other people, other people like Clara Candlewick, who are so, well, they have a better disposition!"

Madeleine stared at Alfred. Did he just say she did not have a pleasant disposition? And who was Clara Candlewick?

Alfred stalked out of the receiving room.

Madeleine felt as if she had been slapped. How dare Alfred, of all fools, insult her? And for what cause? She had done nothing to him. She felt herself flush as she thought of all the barbs she had sent in his direction. Had he noted them? She had not thought so at the time. She had not meant to insult him, exactly. It had only been for her own amusement.

Madeleine felt tears spring to her eyes. First Juliana. Now Alfred. They were the silliest of people. How dare they disdain her? She must see Godfrey. At least he could be trusted. She rose to explore the house and discover the kitchens.

Madeleine found a door leading out of the back of the house. The yard was quiet, not like the castle at all, which always crowded with people and animals. She poked her head around the doorway of the kitchen building.

Godfrey leaned back on a chair, his feet up to the fire in the hearth. "Been my experience, ain't no miller in all Danglen what can be trusted. Thieves, every one."

The cook, a large woman with a red, round face, stood with her hands on her enormous hips. "Insult me man one more time and ya won' be seein' no more ale from me."

Madeleine slipped into the kitchen. The cook saw her and quickly curtsied. "I see you are making friends, Godfrey," she said.

Godfrey sat up and waved his hands. "Agatha don't pay me no mind. We just be jawin' to pass the time."

Madeleine was so used to seeking out Godfrey in the castle's kitchens. She felt awkward standing there in someone else's. She knew Agatha would think it strange that a lady of the house wanted to talk to a servant as a friend. She stood there, not knowing what exactly to say.

Godfrey said, "Aggy, good woman, me and the Lady Madeleine got some business to discuss."

Agatha looked at Madeleine. Madeleine stammered, "Business. Yes. We do."

Agatha said, "Awright. I s'pose I can go have a look in the market." She untied her apron and rumbled out of the kitchen.

Madeleine sat down next to Godfrey.

"Well?" he asked. "What be on yer mind?"

Madeleine was not sure where to start. She had really just come so Godfrey could tell her that all was as it should be. As it had always been. She said, "Do you think me smug?"

"Smug? Who be callin' ye smug?"

"Juliana."

Godfrey nodded. "Well, 'tis hard not to be smug near yer sister. I find it a chore meself."

Madeleine started. "So you think I am?"

122

Godfrey laughed. "Not to me, you ain't. I be sayin' something 'bout it if ya were."

It was not the answer she had been looking for. Or had expected.

"Godfrey."

"Aye."

"Alfred said he does not like my disposition. He compares me to some Clara Candlewick person."

Godfrey nodded. "Aye."

"What does that mean? Aye?"

Godfrey sat up and stretched. "Alfred know he be a fool. And he know ye know it."

"So?"

"So, a man like Alfred needs a gal who don't know he's a fool."

"Well," Madeleine sputtered, "what kind of gal would that be?"

Godfrey put his feet back up to the fire and crossed his arms behind his head. "Clara Candlewick, I s'pose."

Madeleine went back to the receiving room feeling worse than when she had left it.

Her mother sailed in, trailed by Juliana. Juliana cried, "Tell her!"

The Baroness, looking extremely pleased with herself, flourished a parchment. "From my dear friend the Countess deBarge. We are expected for a ball this very night."

Juliana jumped up and down. "A ball, a ball, a ball!"

The Baroness said, "It would not at all surprise me to see the King himself. Only the best society is received by the Countess."

Madeleine muttered, "And us."

The Baroness looked at her sharply. "Watch your tongue, miss. You shall not embarrass me in front of the countess."

Madeleine threw her chin up. "I have no interest in being anywhere near the countess. I shall spend a quiet evening here."

"You shall do no such thing. The invitation is for the Baroness de Clare and her daughters. We shall not disappoint."

Madeleine wracked her mind, looking for a way out. She said, "It is just that suddenly my head--"

"Nonsense. Go upstairs. Your uncle has provided us with a lady's maid. She shall see to you."

Madeleine trudged out of the room, with Juliana skipping behind her. The Baroness called, "Madeleine , come down those stairs with a gracious smile and your manners firmly intact."

Juliana grasped Madeleine's hand and pulled her up the stairs. She chattered all the way up. "You see, Madeleine, we are invited to the best places. I knew it would be so. How silly of you to think we would not. I am sure I shall see Richard there. And I shall be in a new gown. The pale blue velvet suits me, do not you think?"

"Everything suits you," Madeleine mumbled.

Juliana sighed as she pulled Madeleine into their spacious bedchamber. "Must you be cross every day of your life?"

Madeleine had heard enough insults for one day. She felt her temper rolling through her like thunder on an August evening. "Yes. Indeed I must. You would be quite cross if you were me. My own sister thinks I am smug. That I deserve no better than Alfred. Oh, and Alfred thinks Clara somebody has a better disposition!"

"Who is Clara?"

Madeleine felt tears spring to her eyes, though she could not have said why. She really did not care about Alfred and his paramour Clara. It was just that the world did not feel steady under her feet anymore.

"Madeleine, what is wrong with you?"

She heaved a sob. "Everything, apparently." She threw herself on the bed and buried her face into the counterpane.

Juliana stroked her hair. "Come now. I should not have said you deserved Alfred. I am only surprised you even noted something I said."

Madeleine rolled over. "Have I really been that horrid to you?"

Juliana looked away. "A bit. But then, I decided long ago that I could not be as clever as you. So I just ignored you." Juliana looked back at her. "Perhaps it was not very nice, but really, what else could I do?"

Madeleine did not answer. She did not know what else Juliana could have done.

Juliana said, "Enough of this. It is not a night to be sad. We are to go to a ball."

Madeleine sniffled. She sat up and straightened her gown. "You are right. Mother is right. I shall stop acting like a baby this instant. I shall dress and smile and bring my manners firmly intact."

Two hours later, they descended the stairs. The Baroness was dressed in lilac velvet with a matching barbette covering her hair. Juliana wore her cornflower blue gown, her blond curls cascading down from the silver circlet on her head.

The servants had lined up to see them off. They smiled and clapped politely as the two women descended the stairs.

Madeleine had hesitated. She had promised she would pick up her spirits for the ball. She still hadn't found a way to do it. It would be a tedious evening, but she must go all the same. She took a deep breath and walked to the top of the stairs.

The chattering servants fell silent. She gathered the train of her gown. Why do they stare so? I cannot equal Juliana, no one would expect it of me. But I am not a dragon.

She reached the bottom of the stairs. Godfrey leaned in, his breath heavy with ale. "Ya look well."

Alfred held his arm out, but did not look at her.

The carriage ride was not long. The Countess did not rent a house, she had built her own. And she, like so many in fashionable society, had built outside the city walls. The Countess was close enough to arrive at court within an hour's notice, but well away from the filth and stench of the city.

The great iron gates were thrown open. A long avenue overhung with lime trees and oaks was lit at intervals with flaming torches. Carriage after carriage pulled up to the entrance. The carriages were painted in a rainbow of colors with the arms of their owners, and accompanied by coachmen in an array of elaborate liveries. The de Clares appeared to be the only guests in a rented carriage.

The entrance was lit with a hundred torches; Madeleine thought it seemed as daylight. All was so bright and glittering, Madeleine felt she could hardly get her bearings. Alfred had bounded ahead of her, craning his neck and looking over the crowd. Madeleine was moved along with the mass of people, hardly knowing where she was headed.

Her mother touched her arm. "Madeleine. The Countess deBarge."

Madeleine snapped to attention. In front of her was a woman of fifty or so, heavily painted and stuffed into a violet silk gown.

The Countess deBarge eyed Madeleine from head to toe. She smiled and snapped her fan shut. "Charming."

Madeleine curtsied low.

The Countess raised her up. She spoke to the Baroness as if Madeleine were not standing there. "She is unusually striking, my dear," the Countess said to the Baroness. "I predict she shall be quite the sensation. Striking has become all the rage these days."

The Baroness looked at Madeleine as if she had never seen her before.

Madeleine looked past her mother to see Juliana's reaction. Juliana was no longer there.

The Countess had turned to greet other guests. The Baroness said, "Where on earth has Juliana gone off to?"

Madeleine suspected her sister was shamelessly searching the ball for Sir Richard. She said, "She must be with Alfred."

The Baroness nodded absentmindedly and led them into the great hall.

Madeleine had spent hours upon hours imagining what a Bellham ball would be like. Her imagination had fallen far short. The Countess' great hall made the hall at de Clare castle seem an insignificant receiving room. Madeleine stood at one end of a long, rectangular room that seemed to go for leagues. Massive chandeliers hung at intervals, hundreds of beeswax tapers burning brightly. The de Clare's had one hearth that sat central in the hall. The countess had several of the new style, lined against the walls and with chimneys to release the smoke. Hundreds of people milled about, with a lively group of dancers gathering in the middle.

The lute players struck up their tune and the center began to move. Young couples, glowing and giggling, began to dance. Madeleine watched them with interest. Long ago, when she was a small girl, they had employed a dancing master. But she did not recognize the steps.

"What dance is this?" Madeleine asked her mother.

The Baroness did not answer; she was laughing and talking to the woman next to her.

An old man to her left leaned over. "It is the pavan. Too much for these old bones." He pointed to a far corner of the hall. "But if you have a mind to learn it, I see some young ladies over yonder who have found themselves willing teachers."

Madeleine craned her neck. Tucked in a corner, behind trestle tables laden with food, a group of young people laughed and practiced steps. She saw the top of a blond head of curls twirl in a circle. And then, Sir Richard. Saints! Juliana had found him already. Madeleine was surprised that Juliana would be so brazen. She would have thought her sister far more likely to stand about looking pretty until Sir Richard had discovered her. Apparently, Juliana had decided to leave nothing to chance.

Madeleine stepped in front of the Baroness' view just as her mother turned to view the dance floor.

The Baroness looked around. Madeleine did her best to move with her to block her view of Juliana. "Good Heavens, you are as jumpy as a cat," her mother said. "Where is Alfred? Why do you not dance with him?"

Madeleine shrugged, still trying to stay in front of the Baroness.

"Stay still for a moment. What in heavens..."

Madeleine had not been fast enough. The Baroness stared at the dance floor. Madeleine slowly turned around.

Juliana and Sir Richard had moved to the center of the hall. They glided down a line of couples. Sir Richard wore a silly grin and Juliana looked as if she floated above the floor.

The Baroness pressed her lips together. "Sir Richard. That can only mean the earl is not far behind."

Madeleine felt her stomach flip. She had convinced herself that it would not be so. The earl could not be recovered enough to attend a ball. She scanned the room. He was tall enough, he would not be hard to find. Relief and disappointment flooded through her at the same time. He was not there.

"I may just have a word with Beaumont when I see him. His rudeness was inexcusable." The Baroness said.

"No!" Madeleine cried.

Her mother looked at her as if she had lost her wits.

"I mean, certainly," Madeleine said, "we must pretend we did not even note his departure. We must not give him the satisfaction of believing it had any effect on us. And surely he is still abed recovering from his injury."

The Baroness looked unconvinced. Madeleine said, "Perhaps he did not even survive the journey," hoping that might cheer her mother.

The Baroness considered this. "I hardly think Sir Richard would be here, were the earl in any danger. Well, I suppose we must appear dignified." She glanced at Juliana again. "Though I do not think I like the attention Sir Richard pays to Juliana. He is overly bold."

Madeleine laughed. "Oh, Sir Richard is quite harmless. Just a convenient dancing partner." She took her mother by the arm. "Come and let us have some spiced wine; it is hot in here."

"Yes, indeed it is. And perhaps we shall find Alfred."

Madeleine escorted her mother to one of the smaller receiving rooms to get refreshment. It was far cooler than the great hall; the leaded panes had been removed from one of the windows to let fresh air in.

The room was filled with an older crowd who no longer found dancing an entertainment. Two ancient men sat hunched over a chessboard, staring at the pieces as if they might get up and move themselves. Several groups of ladies chattered and fanned themselves. Servants glided silently about the room, offering ale, cider and mulled wine. Madeleine's mother seemed to know everybody.

Madeleine was introduced, scrutinized, poked, and prodded. One large lady exclaimed, "Is this the one we hear so much about?"

The Baroness laughed. "No, that is Juliana. She is in the hall dancing. You must see her before evening's end."

The large lady said, "Well, you have had real luck with your daughters if the other is prettier than this."

Madeleine flushed. The Baroness stammered, "Yes, indeed." For the second time in one night, she looked at Madeleine as if she had never seen her before.

The conversation dropped into silence. Then her mother cried, "Ah! There he is."

Madeleine froze. It could not be.

Madeleine turned around. It was only Alfred. Yet again, she had forgotten his very existence.

Alfred stood in a corner, his head bent over a young woman. The girl had light brown curls rolling in circles down her back. She looked up at Alfred with large brown eyes. Madeleine thought there was something strangely like admiration in those eyes.

Her mother had her by the arm, propelling her across the room.

"Alfred, my dear, where have you been hiding?"

Alfred looked up, startled. "Oh, I, no, I did not hide..."

"I do not believe we have met your friend," the Baroness said, scrutinizing the young lady.

"Oh! Yes. Of course. The Baroness de Clare, Lady Madeleine de Clare, pleased to introduce Miss Clara Candlewick."

Madeleine stifled a gasp. So this was she of the better disposition.

Clara Candlewick curtsied gracefully. She rose and smiled.

Madeleine looked at her more closely. She was round in every aspect. Her round face with its round brown eyes and round little mouth struck Madeleine as both odd and appealing. She looked as gentle as a newborn calf.

"Alfred, as much as I hate to disappoint a young lady by depriving her of your company," the Baroness said, "remember your promise to dance with Madeleine."

Clara Candlewick flushed and looked away.

The Baroness stared hard at Alfred. "Yes, I am sorry Miss Candlewick, my nephew has a prior commitment."

Alfred's mouth worked as if he might say something, but nothing came out. Clara Candlewick looked as if she would like to disappear through the floor.

"I am sorry, mother. That is impossible," Madeleine said. She winked at Alfred. "I have quite the headache."

Alfred started. "You do?"

Madeleine nodded at him, smiling. "Terrible."

Clara Candlewick peeked out from her curls.

"Madeleine," the Baroness said in a hiss.

Alfred said, "Feel better, then." He grabbed Clara Candlewick's arm and dragged her from the room.

Madeleine waited for her mother's tirade, but she found she really did not care. She would marry Alfred, but had just lately found she was not the only one who would be miserable over it. He should have at least one night of happiness. Alfred was in love with Clara Candlewick.

Chapter Fifteen – The Countess deBarge's Ball

The Baroness glared at Madeleine . "You do not have a headache!"

Madeleine smiled. "No. I do not."

"How dare you...you cannot just--"

"But I just did."

The Baroness' face grew twisted and red.

Juliana bounced in front of them from nowhere. "Madeleine, come now, Sir Richard insists on a dance." She pecked her mother's cheek. "Good Heavens mother, sit and cool yourself, you are as purple as the King's cloak." She grabbed Madeleine's hand and pulled her away.

Madeleine let herself be led. Dancing was the second to last thing she wanted to do. But the very last was to stay in the vicinity of her enraged mother.

Juliana wove her in and around the crowd and back into the great hall. It was even more crowded now. The room had filled to capacity and was heated from a hundred bodies dancing.

Juliana pulled her through rows of dancers. She stopped in the middle. "Just here. Richard said he would meet us just here."

Dancers glided past them in all directions. "Just here?" Madeleine asked. "Juliana, we are in everyone's way."

Juliana did not answer. She scanned the room for Sir Richard. She looked over Madeleine's head and smiled. "Here we are." She took Madeleine by the shoulders and spun her around.

Sir Richard had Lord Beaumont by the shoulders. He said, "Juliana insists on one dance with you. Do not be tedious." He spun the earl around.

Beaumont turned with a look of impatience on his face. He looked at Juliana and forced a smile. He saw Madeleine and his smile faded.

"Come Richard, we have done our charity for one night," Juliana said.

Juliana and Sir Richard disappeared into the crowd of dancers.

Madeleine felt as if the world had disappeared. She knew there were hundreds of people swirling around her, yet she could hardly hear the music. Beaumont stood before her as tall and handsome as ever. He seemed none the worse for Alfred's assault. What should she say? She must say something.

Beaumont bowed.

Madeleine curtsied. She stammered, "You are well."

"Yes."

She gazed around the room, searching her mind for words. Simple words! She usually had so many of them. Too many of them. She blurted, "Alfred is here."

The earl's face tightened. He looked over her head. "Convey my felicitations. Excuse me." He turned on his heel and was gone in the sea of people.

Madeleine stood alone in the vast crowd. What had just happened? Her stomach lurched. Beaumont must think she and Alfred formally engaged. Why else would she make a point of mentioning him? Why had she? Why did that man always make her say something she had no intention of saying?

Madeleine felt the eyes of the dancers that twirled by her. How ridiculous she must look, standing alone in the middle of the dance. Her face grew hot as she thought of how many people must have seen her with the earl. And seen him stalk away and leave her stranded. Where was Juliana? She had to get out of this place.

Tears started in Madeleine's eyes; the hall swam in front of her in a salty sea. How could he leave her there, looking like such an idiot? Beaumont must hate her indeed.

She swiped her eyes. The dance was coming to an end. As soon as it did, Madeleine would run from this place.

"I cannot go before I speak my mind."

Beaumont stood before her again. Was he trying to make her the most miserable person on earth?

She waved her hand. "You have made me look the biggest of fools. You have your revenge. Just go."

He mumbled something unintelligible.

Madeleine stamped her foot. "What!"

Beaumont raised his voice over the crowd. "I shall be heard!"

The dancers nearest them stopped and stared. The lute players trailed off to silence. Like a ripple through a pond, the hall grew quiet around them.

Madeleine glared at the earl. Did he mean to shame her in front of hundreds of people?

Beaumont glanced at the silent crowd. He paled and took a deep breath. "I am too proud and stubborn." He cleared his throat. "As are you."

She felt her temper rise. She would not be so humiliated. Wait. Had he just said he was too proud and stubborn?

"I have believed a proper wife would have certain attributes. That you do not have."

It was never enough for this man! He would ruin her name in front of all of Bellham!

Beaumont shuffled his feet. "A mild manner, agreeable disposition, gentle demeanor...so on and so forth. In short, the things that you are not."

Madeleine heard a giggle behind her. It sounded suspiciously like Juliana. Would no one come to her defense? Where was her mother when she was truly needed?

"You are too opinionated," the earl continued. "Too sharp in manner. Too temperamental. But the fact is, since I met you, I have had to reconsider my requirements. It is my unfortunate fate to have fallen in love. With you. So, I must marry you or no one."

The crowd gasped.

The earl turned various shades of red. "You cannot marry Alfred."

Madeleine wanted to slap him. Then laughter bubbled around her insides. She threw her chin up. "You are too disagreeable. Too haughty. Too...blond. It would not be harmonious. We would have many disagreements."

"Yes."

"We would have proud and disagreeable children that we should not know what to do with. And I cannot even imagine how tall they would be."

"No doubt."

"It is too ridiculous. There is simply everything against it."

"Absolutely."

Madeleine shrugged. "As long as you are forewarned."

"Completely. Is it yes, then?"

Madeleine took a breath. "Yes."

The people around her cheered and clapped. A man to her left called to the back of the crowd. "She says yes!"

Beaumont leaned over and whispered in Madeleine's ear. "Let us leave before I die of embarrassment."

He earl clasped Madeleine's hand and led her through the crowd, ignoring his well-wishers. Madeleine trailed behind him in a happy daze. How had this happened? How had any of it happened? How had Juliana become clever? And Madeleine not so clever? How had Alfred found his true love? How was it that Madeleine truly wished him well? Madeleine was startled out of her reverie. Beaumont had stopped abruptly, and she crashed into his back.

In front of Madeleine , the earl said, "M'lady, I have asked your daughter for her hand. She has accepted. May I presume you have no objection?"

Madeleine heard her mother gasp. Then she said, "Oh! Naturally. I wondered at a man able to resist Juliana. It seemed so unnatural, I should have realized--"

"Not Juliana, you daft woman. Madeleine."

"Oh?"

Madeleine pecked her mother's cheek as she walked by. She called over her shoulder, "Juliana shall marry Sir Richard, mother. And you shall be happy for her."

"What?"

Beaumont led Madeleine out onto a veranda. The air was crisp and the stars were sharp white.

"I came against my will tonight," Madeleine said. "I did not think you would be here."

Beaumont laughed. "I came against my will also. Your cousin's aim still aches. My physician said I must not rise from bed under any circumstances. Richard called him an old woman, threw him from the house and threw me into a carriage."

"But how did Sir Richard know that Juliana would be here?"

Beaumont flushed.

Madeleine threw her chin up. "Lord?"

"Well, he may have had a private conversation with my brother. Who may have been employed to keep watch on de Clare castle. After delivering a token of my esteem."

"The silver!"

"Yes."

"I wondered....a rose with no thorns is no rose at all."

"Making you very rosy, indeed."

Before Madeleine could answer, he pulled her into his arms. He said, "Now, you have just engaged yourself to a haughty earl. My first haughty command is you must call me Henry."

Madeleine said, "I shall agree to that, only to be agreeable."

"I would also insist that when I am being particularly disagreeable, you must note it."

"And when I am being particularly disagreeable, you must note it as well," Madeleine said.

"I fear we shall spend a good deal of our lives noting."

Madeleine laughed. "And we must hire Godfrey as our cook. Then when we have both been disagreeable, we may insult his cooking, thereby agreeing on something. I am sure he shall not mind it."

"He is a perfectly ridiculous cook. And so, perfect for us."

THE END

Made in the USA
Columbia, SC
21 August 2020